RESURRECTION SPELLS FOR THE DEAD RELATIONSHIP

SULA ALBA

To my great-grandmother Sultana.

I hope you don't mind I named myself after you.

CONTENT NOTES

This paranormal romance book features on-page steamy scenes. It does also touch on several sensitive topics and themes. If you'd like to know more you can find a full list on my website: https://www.sulaalba.com/content-warnings

Take care and happy reading!

Chapter One

Ellie Rodriguez dragged her boyfriend's dead body into her apartment. She dragged him by his feet, heaving harder as he slowed down on her carpet. She could swear that he was heavier now than when he was alive. Dead bodies weighed more than live ones. Her mother's limbs weighed her down like anchors after she passed. Ellie remembered holding her for twenty minutes before the ambulance came. What would she think about her daughter now? As she dragged Derek's lifeless body through her living room. His head bounced off the coffee table leg. Ellie winced, but she couldn't do more damage to a dead man, anyway.

Ellie used her last bit of strength to haul him into the middle of the living room. She tried to arrange his body in a better position, moving his arms down by his sides and his hips in line with his torso, but he was so stiff already. His limbs refused to cooperate.

She arranged white taper candles around his body. She stuck the candles on melted puddles of wax. Her shaking hands made the work tedious. What should have taken five minutes took twenty.

This was not supposed to happen.

Someone discovering her boyfriend's dead body in the woods was not supposed to happen. Having to break into the morgue, drag his body into her car, and into her second-story apartment was not supposed to happen. There were many unplanned events in Ellie's life that weren't supposed to happen. Each successive disaster made her more frazzled and emotional than the last. Her life was one tragedy after another, but this was one tragedy too far.

Derek had been missing for two days. Two days she had spent calling his phone almost every ten minutes with no answer. She called his work, his friends; she would have called his family, but he never did get around to introducing her to his family. Ellie's mind ran with every fear she had felt her entire life. Derek abandoned her. Returned to his secret family in another state. He never loved her; it was all a lie, and he replaced her with a blond bombshell from Russia. The truth was far worse.

She had watched the ten o'clock news as they described joggers finding a man dead in the woods. The killer hadn't buried the body. They described a six-foot-tall man with blond hair, blue eyes, age around thirty. Ellie's heart sank at the news, as the police asked for tips and help from the public. Her palms became itchy, and later that day she found a dead crow on the hood of her car. She knew it was Derek.

Ellie cried while mixing the anointment. She kept her eyes away from the mixture. This was a delicate procedure. If she wasn't careful, any unknown ingredient could alter the spell. She tiptoed around the lit candles, avoiding the wet wax pooling on the floor.

How long did it take for dead bodies to decompose? She didn't know, but she tried not to think about it. His body was developing a smell, but it wasn't a rotten stench yet. She looked through the ingredients she bought in a hurry; she didn't keep a stocked apothecary. Even then, *yew*? She'd never heard of the herb before, but she was lucky enough to find it on such short notice.

She double-checked the instructions written in an unknown script in her mother's spell book. As the mixture thickened, the herbs mixed with the oils, and it became difficult to stir. But there was one ingredient still missing. She reached for the kitchen knife near Derek's head.

Blood.

For a serious spell like this, it always required blood.

She tried not to think of the pain as she positioned the cool edge on her palm. She took a deep breath and closed her hand around the blade. Something in her moved then, a heaviness in her stomach bubbling up with dread and nausea, screaming at her to wait.

Her hands drifted to his face, trying in vain to fix his hair over his bloodied skull. His skin was gray and pallid, drained of all that she loved about him. The harsh black stitches she'd sewn on his chest at the morgue stood in sharp contrast with his pale skin. She tried to hold back the bile, thinking about it. She had gotten to the morgue in time, before the examination began. Before all his organs were chopped up and placed inside a plastic bag. His organs were intact, but someone had butterflied him open, and Ellie cursed herself for going to law school and not medical school.

She checked her stitches. A few had loosened somewhere along the chaotic transportation. She had tried her best to stretch his skin to cover the paling gray organs. Did skin shrink in death? Ellie thought it might have. She'd pierced his flesh with a curved needle left out by a forgetful medical examiner, and she stitched him together again. Her hope and resolve solidified with each crooked stitch.

How could someone kill him? Where was his killer now? She pushed the thoughts away. She assured herself they would have time to find his killer together; to seek justice for the murder of the man she loved. She couldn't wait to cast her spell, not for a second longer.

Ellie pulled the knife against her tightly closed palm. She cried out from the pain as her blood dripped into the bowl. She wasn't sure how much she needed. The book hadn't specified the amount; it only said *sangre*. She whisked the blood into the mixture, holding her bleeding palm up to not drip on the floor. After she was done, she reminded herself to throw out the whisk later. She peered down at the book and held her non-injured hand over the bowl. She recited the spell. Her Spanish sounded garbled to her, shaky with sobs that hadn't stopped for days. She needed to concentrate. She repeated the spell, her voice steadying long enough to recite the incantation before the shakiness returned.

For a moment, nothing happened. The seconds ticked on, and Ellie's sobs grew more desperate. Until her fingertips tingled with sharp pops. A sweet heat, which she didn't always appreciate, followed. The heat traveled to her palms, and she dipped her hands into the bowl, scooping some of the mixture into her cupped hands.

This will work, she told herself. *It has to.*

She smeared the anointing on his skin. Her fingers brushed skin that felt like cold stone, but the heat from her palms left a faint trace of warmth. She covered his entire body, willing her spell to work, reassured by the pink left behind by her hands. It could have been the low light, or the pink of her diluted blood, but she inspected the skin. No, it was his skin returning to the land of the living. She prayed his soul would soon follow.

She took the last of the mixture and let her fingers graze his cheeks. His stubble pricked her fingertips, and her eyes went to the wound on his head. The blood had long dried, plastering his hair to his forehead. She kissed his stiff lips as she finished spreading the rest of the mixture on his forehead.

She sat up and waited. The apartment's silence lay heavy on Ellie's anxiety. Was she too late? She looked at his body. The traces of the pink warmth she left were fading. Her tears were welling up again. She failed.

She had no one to blame but herself. It had been years since she cast and resurrection spells took tremendous power. She was delusional for thinking she could do it.

Ellie sat down, folding her legs to her chest and pressing her forehead to her knees. Her sobs flowed mercilessly through her, and she felt powerless to stop them.

She gripped her legs, trying to stifle her shaking, when her body froze. A cold sensation passed through her, causing her breathing to stop mid-gasp. For a moment, she felt like she sat in a freezer naked. Her bones shook and her teeth chattered. But as soon as the cold arrived, it left.

She looked down at Derek. He looked the same. She kneeled closer, watching his chest for any sign of movement, but he lay still. Her eyes traveled down his arms to the tips of his fingers. She gasped, noticing the faint pink on his nail beds. Relief washed through her as she watched the color spread. First through his hands, up his arms, soon his feet and legs were returning to their original color, too. When the flush reached his heart, his body responded by taking a gasping breath. She jumped back, startled, as his chest heaved upwards. Derek's body fell, shaking the dirty mugs on the coffee table near him.

She waited, watching his chest move up and down. She dared not touch him. Derek opened his eyes. He looked around frantically, his blue eyes taking in the surroundings until they settled on her. Ellie expected him to calm down when his eyes landed on her, but he didn't.

He looked down at his body and retched.

"Ellie, what the hell is this?" She didn't blame him for freaking out.

He continued looking at his naked body, and Ellie noticed his head wound had completely healed. Derek pulled at the stitches on his chest. He pulled the string hard, wincing as it snapped. His organs were probably fine, reasoned Ellie. She wanted to touch him, but she stopped herself.

"What the hell happened? And what the hell is this?" He struggled to wipe the dried anointment off his skin. Herbs fell in flakes to the floor.

There was no use hiding it now. She never told him she was a witch. It was a dangerous thing to admit. Especially with the witch hunts occurring around the country for the past four years. She hadn't considered this in her plan. It had frankly surprised her that it had worked at all.

"I brought you back from the dead."

"What?" He stopped trying to wipe away the anointment and stared at her. His eyes conveyed a mixture of confusion and hurt.

"You were dead. They found you in the woods with your skull bashed open. And I didn't know what else to do."

Derek stayed quiet, turning away from her. She tried to gauge his reaction, but he proved hard to read. Their third-year anniversary was coming up, and she had kept the biggest secret from him.

"Please say something," she finally said.

"How?"

"I cast a spell to bring you back to life. I'm a witch. I've been a witch my whole life. I never told you because I don't practice. At least not since my mom…" She couldn't finish the sentence.

Derek looked stunned, and she couldn't imagine what thoughts ran through his head. The uncomfortable truth was she never told him because she was afraid. Afraid of being turned in by the one person she loved the most. She feared another witch trial, where they would parade her in front of the cameras and the public. He loved her; she was sure of it, but would he love her despite what she'd hidden from him?

Derek looked at her again, and where Ellie hoped to find a sympathetic gaze or one of hate, was instead strangely blank.

"Are you okay?" she asked.

"Never felt better." He stretched out his arms and smelled one of his hands. "God, I reek. I need a shower. We'll talk later, okay?" He stood up, his legs shaky.

He'd been dead for three days.

CHAPTER TWO

Ellie thought it was weird that a man brought back from the dead didn't have more questions. She watched him during the morning, waiting for the inevitable questions. But he sang in the shower and whistled while he cooked breakfast for them.

It was normal-ish.

Shouldn't he be a little more freaked?

She downed her third cup of coffee and watched him flip the eggs. Maybe it was her own nerves talking. In the past three days, she'd only slept ten hours.

He sat down next to her, and his arm brushed against hers. His skin still felt cold.

"How are you feeling?" she asked.

"Great." He took a bite of his toast but noticed her staring. "Honestly, Ellie, I feel good."

"Do you remember what happened the night you died?"

"When was that again?" he said it like he was trying to remember what he had for breakfast.

"Three nights ago."

"I remember going to Paradise, the bar near Franklin Street."

She knew it. Some of her classmates at school had invited her to go out for a drink with them a few times. She always said no, not to be rude, but law school students could be snobs. She spoke to a few of them during class and her internship, but she liked to keep to herself.

"Then what happened?" she asked.

"I drank? And then... I remember nothing after that."

"Were you drugged?"

"I'm not sure."

"There's nothing else?"

"No, I mean, everything's fuzzy. I've tried to remember, but honestly, nothing comes back. I remember having a few drinks and then I woke up covered in that gunk on the floor."

"It might come back later," said Ellie hopefully.

He shrugged, uninterested in it.

Ellie convinced herself it was fine. Maybe even a normal reaction. If someone had murdered her, she wouldn't be too eager to get those memories back, either.

"You don't have questions for me?" she asked.

"What do you mean?" His fingers traced her arm, and she shivered at his icy fingers.

"I mean, I told you I'm a witch. That's not exactly a popular thing to be right now."

Not since the government outlawed witchcraft. The change in federal law occurred four years ago. When the government ruled that witchcraft was not a real religion, the First Amendment didn't protect its practitioners. Real religions, they argued, had doctrine. A book that all members of any religion could agree upon to follow. Witches were eclectic, most only having a book of shadows passed down through each generation. It didn't qualify in their eyes.

Next came the accusations. Sure, a preacher could ask the pulpit for God's wrath to punish certain enemies. All that was fine; it was God's will and correct. Yet, if a witch cursed someone, then it became a problem. Witches acted under the influence and power of evil. Soon, those accusations were fodder for hysteria, and the governing bodies saw fit to restore order by punishing the accused.

Murder by witchcraft became a popular crime to accuse someone of. Did they discover the deceased in a bedroom with candles? Did the accused person wear black and listen to 'dark' music? Were there carvings on the walls or on the body itself that called upon Satan? Did children learn about spells and rituals in daycare and school? Everything seemed to lead to witchcraft, and the law caused chaos.

Witches went into hiding then, at least the lucky ones did. The police received reports from the enemies of the unlucky ones as soon as the protections lifted. Regular mortals with no powers or casting ability at all were the unluckiest. The police hunted and tried them alongside the genuine witches.

"I won't tell anyone you're a witch, Ellie. I mean, not after what you did for me."

"So would you have turned me in if you had known before?"

"Of course not." He grabbed her face between his hands and kissed her. There he was, the Derek she loved. The Derek that held her close at night and made her feel whole. After all these days of torment, she could finally see him. "I would never have turned you in. But do you even trust me if you kept this secret from me for almost three years?"

"I'm sorry. I should have told you sooner." He looked hurt, and the gnawing guilt crept into Ellie's heart.

He let go of her face and continued eating. She ate the eggs he made for her, but her mind raced again. Not that she didn't want to tell him, but something had always kept her from disclosing it. An instinct of sorts. She never felt safe enough to tell anyone, including Derek. Admitting it to someone was dangerous, and she wanted to stay alive as long as possible.

There had already been a few near misses. A glance from a stranger when she pulled out some money for a tip at a coffee shop and a bay leaf fell out. A cop stared at her as three crows landed by her feet one day outside the library. Every moment led Ellie into a spiral of overthinking. Wondering if it was enough for an accusation. She had hidden well enough for the past few years, but resurrecting Derek had been the biggest risk she'd ever taken. She tried not to consider the many missed steps or forgotten ends that could now lead to her discovery.

The rest of the morning passed by in silence. She wanted to sleep, but she kept observing Derek. She looked for issues. Anything that she could have done wrong, but everything appeared fine.

Then why did something seem off to her? Why couldn't she relax and enjoy her recently resurrected boyfriend?

"Don't you have class today?" he asked while he flipped through the channels on TV.

"Yeah, but I figured I should stay."

"Why?"

"To stay with you, just in case."

"I'm fine."

"Someone did murder you. What if they tried again?"

"Well, they don't know I'm alive, right? Why would they be looking?" He had a point there. "Come on, get ready. I'll drop you. On the way back, we can pick up my car from the impound."

"There's no way you're driving me."

"Why?" he asked.

"Derek, you were dead. The police probably knew a little about you, even if they didn't have your identity. It'll be suspicious if they catch a dead man driving. They might figure out it was I who brought you back."

"Please, nobody actually believes there are actual witches, Ellie. I mean, I never thought there were. Clearly, I was wrong. But I won't stay cooped up at home when you gave me a second chance at life."

He got up and wrapped his arms around her, bringing her in close to his chest. He still felt cold, and Ellie shivered against his chest. Strange to think a few hours ago she had cried as she tried to pull his skin taut to stitch his chest together. It already seemed like a lifetime ago.

She breathed him in; she had made the right decision. A life without him would've been unbearable. "I don't think you'll be able to go back to your old life without exposing me as a witch."

"You didn't think that far ahead, did you?"

"To be honest, I'm surprised it even worked." He chuckled, making her smile.

"I'll go back to my normal life."

"Derek, no…" she opened her mouth to protest, but he put a finger on her lips.

"I'm going to, Ellie," he said. His tone lowered, and Ellie's heart skipped a beat. "If I get questions, I'll tell them they made a mistake. That wasn't me. I just came back from a trip. The witches they catch are just fake psychics peddling scams, that's all. They don't know real witchcraft. I didn't know what real, powerful witchcraft was until today. They won't figure it out. I'll outsmart them like I do everyone else."

Ellie's unease didn't dissipate. What she wanted to do was transfer to another law school and finish her degree in a different town. She would help Derek adopt a new identity. Despite the risk that the police had observed his dead body, Derek disregarded her plans. She reminded herself that had been one of the things she had liked about him when they first started dating. He had a plan for everything.

But she didn't want to go to class or work. Even if she had already missed three days from her internship at the law offices of Nelson and Johnson. What she wanted to do was sleep, but she didn't have a choice in the matter. "I'll just get ready." She heard him mumble 'perfect' as she left to the bathroom.

She gazed at herself in the mirror and thought she looked closer to death now than Derek had when he was actually dead. Her brown eyes appeared sunken thanks to the bags under her eyes. She was due for an appointment with her eyebrow lady, and her dark hair lay flat and limp. She had no clue how she was going to stay awake during class.

She tried her best to look presentable after a shower. When she left her room, Derek was by the door, holding her backpack. They climbed into her car and drove down to campus. They were silent the whole car ride, and she fell asleep on the passenger side.

A hand nudged her awake a few minutes later. She started to get out, but Derek grabbed her hand and pulled her close. They kissed, his lips smashing into hers. She froze, taken aback, and as much as she tried to fall into the kiss, her heart skipped. His kiss was different. Harsh, forceful, and hurried.

He pulled away. If he noticed a difference, he said nothing. "I'll pick you up later. Have a good day."

Ellie gave a half-hearted smile and stepped out of the car. As she slung her backpack over her shoulder, she found two people staring at her.

One person she knew, Violet Caldwell, one of her classmates. She looked upset, but when Ellie made eye contact with her, she turned and walked towards class. Ellie had never seen the other person before. His tall frame stood still, blocking the entrance. His brow furrowed as he stared at her. Ellie noticed his brown eyes on her, but he didn't look away as she drew closer. He dropped his binders, and the trance broke. He stumbled to gather all the papers flying around him. She stooped to help him. He had beautiful long fingers, and he snatched the papers, crumpling some of them in his haste. She handed him some papers, and he paled.

Like he had seen a ghost.

Chapter Three

River saw a dead man. Alive, driving no less. He was supposed to be dead. At least he had been the night before. River was sure of it because he'd opened his chest only a few hours ago. Yet there he was in the car. Dangling one of his arms out the window. His head was no longer bloody or bashed in.

River fumbled with the binders in his hands, dropping them. He was late to the one class he taught at the university as an adjunct. Forensic Anthropology, a master's level course for the morbidly curious. The police had delayed him in the morning, throwing his entire schedule off. A body disappeared in the night, a body he had prepped for examination. It took a while for River to get to the dead man's body because of the backlog of people he had to examine. It seemed the police and unsuspecting people found at least two to three people dead in the woods every day lately.

River finished clocking-in when his colleague Brian, sweating and talking a mile a minute, told him about what he had discovered that morning.

"It's gone!" Brian yelled.

"What's gone?" River asked, jarred by Brian's frantic energy so early in the morning.

"John Doe, 30, the man that came in a day ago? Remember?"

"Yeah, I guess I remember. What do you mean, it's gone?"

"I was going to finish examining the young woman from yesterday, and I noticed someone had left one of the body lockers open. I thought it was an accident, and so I went to close it, but I found this." He handed River the body tag.

"Somebody took a body?" asked River. He couldn't even imagine how someone would go about stealing a body from the morgue.

"I checked the security footage this morning, and there's a gap in the recording." They later examined the footage, and there was a missing hour-long chunk from 2:45 am to 3:45 am.

"Who would want to steal a body?" River asked.

"Who do you think? I bet it was a witch." River's spine stiffened.

Sometimes, River forgot Brian was one of the people who were happy about the Witchcraft Exclusion Act. River had never met any witches. He thought them to be fictional, but the news of the witch hunts horrified him. River had joined the protests at the beginning. The early outrage drove thousands out of their homes and into the streets. But the nation moved on, and the Exclusion Act stayed. Everything continued as before, except each week they accused a few dozen people of witchcraft. River thought the world regressed, and it made him angry.

"Do you really think a witch would have done this? Seems like a lot of trouble for just one random dude," River tried to laugh it off.

"They use the body parts in their rituals and eat what's left over." It sounded fake, but River didn't want to point it out. He had his own peculiarities, and he knew if Brian learned of them, it would get him sent into a trial faster than he could yell 'WITCH'.

"We'll make a report with the police, but there isn't much more damage someone can do to a dead body. Hopefully, he'll turn up."

And turned up he had. River saw the girl first coming out of the car. He didn't know what made him look in that direction, other than his 'peculiarity'. Call it instinct, call it vibes, but he sometimes knew things.

He knew the dead man was going to die before he did. River had sat a few stools away from him in Paradise. River watched him hit on a woman with red hair and freckles all over her skin. She giggled obnoxiously, eager no doubt to be talking to a guy so handsome. Yet when the man turned to ask the bartender for another drink, River felt it. This guy, whose name he didn't even know, was going to die soon. He didn't know how; he didn't know how soon, but he was certain.

When his body had reached the morgue and River unzipped his bag, he recognized him right away. Ashy blond hair and an angular nose. It was definitely him, but with a bashed-in head. River would have warned him if he hadn't left with the girl when River had gone to the bathroom, but it was always tricky to let others into his gift. He could never be sure if the person would take the news as a blessing or an omen. He had to be careful. Even if he wasn't a witch, they often grouped psychics with them. He couldn't risk his life like that.

Brian was beside himself, explaining it all to the two police officers. The police's near glee at listening to Brain's story made River uncomfortable. Their pens dashed across their notepads, not missing any of the details Brian gave them. Or maybe River read too much into it. Stealing a dead body was a crime. They would want to get as much information as possible. They weren't looking at a witch as the automatic suspect.

"Did the witch leave anything behind?" One officer asked Brian.

Shit. Never mind.

"Not that I saw, but you're free to look further," Brian said. One officer looked at River. He'd been quiet. Suspiciously quiet? God, he hoped not.

"What about you?"

"What about me?" River wondered whether he sounded too confrontational. He couldn't help himself but question every move in front of the police. Ever since the witch hunts, he had been on edge, wondering if they would use his gift against him. If one of his friends or ex-girlfriends would remember when he knew something before it happened. Would they hate him enough to turn him in, like so many other witches were before him? The trials on television had been excruciating to watch.

Even if the people were witches, they didn't deserve to be treated like animals and paraded on television. River knew, however, that the likelihood of every person they prosecuted being an actual witch was low. How soon until they brought him in front of a jury?

"Did you notice anything unusual or out-of-place today?" asked officer Wharton. He had a paunch belly, and he had tried to comb his few remaining hairs to cover his bald spot.

"I just got here. It was Brian who told me the body was missing."

"Did you examine the body?"

"I was going to examine him today. I prepared the body last night."

"You were the last to see the body."

"I guess I was. I stored it in the body bag and put it in the fridge last night." The police flipped to a new page in their notepad.

"What was the condition of the body?" he asked.

"There was blunt force trauma on the skull, but it didn't seem deep enough to cause his death. I didn't have time to examine his body thoroughly, however, and I wasn't able to send out for the toxicology report yet."

"Why did you wait so long to examine the body?" he asked.

"We've been backed up. Six bodies came in the same day as this man. Some of them were further along in the decay process. They took priority."

"You said the wound wasn't too bad to be his cause of death? So, do you think he just died from natural causes?"

"I can't say that for sure without having examined the body. But on the outside, besides the head wound, there were no other markers of trauma."

"Sounds like a witch's death to me," Brian accused. The police nodded their heads, and River wanted to flee the room.

River grew nervous, his palms sweating, and he didn't understand why. He didn't kill the man. *I basically did*, said a small voice in his head. *By not warning him.* Yet he wasn't sure more could have been done. Would the man have listened?

But the man wasn't dead. River watched as John Doe kissed a girl he dropped off. Dead men didn't just come back to life, and River hated to admit it, but perhaps Brian was right. River studied the man, trying to convince himself that it was a different person. A twin brother, perhaps? Yet something forced his attention elsewhere as the dead man's girl turned towards him.

River felt it then, a pull, almost at the middle of his torso. His peculiarity pushed the dead man out of his mind. She walked towards the building, her long brown hair nearly down to her waist. Her backpack was slung over slender shoulders. He couldn't move from where he stood. His instincts, which he long regarded as a curse, held him fixed on her. He dreaded it, yet it excited him all the same.

Who was she? Why was he drawn to her? Why was she in danger? The last question especially upset him because he knew she was in trouble. Just as he knew, he had to get her away from the dead man.

His thoughts distracted him so much that he didn't feel the binders slip from his fingers. Panicking, River bent down to gather everything, snapping out of his stupor. Another pair of hands helped him pick up the papers. He looked up and saw the woman in front of him. Big brown eyes met his, and his heart skipped a beat. This close to her, River felt the sense stronger now.

She would die soon.

Chapter Four

Six days passed since Derek's resurrection, and Ellie watched for any signs of trouble. She'd never cast such a dangerous spell before. Ellie didn't practice her craft so recklessly. She often stuck a bay leaf in her wallet to attract money. She'd hidden a sigil underneath her car seat to keep her safe while driving. Small bits of protective magic she had watched her mother perform as a child were part of her routine. Yet this? Her mother had never taught her this.

Ellie didn't recognize which of her ancestors had written the spell, but the handwriting was not her mother's. In the days that followed the resurrection, she wondered what her mother would have told her if she'd been alive. She would have stopped her; Ellie was sure of it. But would Ellie have stopped herself?

She wanted to believe she would have made the same choice. She would've brought Derek back, regardless of what her mother said. But the gnawing questions in her head gave her pause. She pushed it aside; she couldn't think like that. Her decision was final, and as she reached out and placed her hand on Derek's back as he slept, she was sure she had made the right choice.

And yet, the burrowing feeling, like a worm trying to tuck itself into the folds of her brain, didn't go away. In the six days post-resurrection, she and Derek discussed her witchcraft. Every question made her fidget. She tried to tell herself it was because she'd been hiding it for so long. She had never told anyone before, even before the ban and the trials. Her mother was old-school like that. Her mother remembered people seeking witches or *cundaderos* in her culture for their specific magical skills. The change in their reputation occurred long before Ellie was born, but her mother was especially attuned to the troubles that were to come.

"Has your spell book been in your family a long time?" asked Derek.

"It goes back at least three generations."

"Is that when your family started practicing witchcraft?"

"I think it was when they first thought it was safe enough to write it down."

"What did they do before then?"

"Pass it orally?"

"You don't know?"

"I never asked."

Ellie didn't realize how many questions she would have after her mother died. She never stopped long enough to think about it too closely. Other feelings took precedence. The physical absence of her mother trumped everything else. She only realized how much she lost five years later. Her mother had been like a living encyclopedia of knowledge. She didn't have to look through the book to know what she needed for a spell or an incantation. It lived within her, and she could wield her powers to do the most beautiful magical things. She wondered what her mother would think if she saw her now. Would she even recognize her? Ellie scarcely recognized herself.

Ellie found herself in some trouble at her internship after her absence. The attorneys had given most of her assignments to the other eager interns, not that she could blame them for it. Her excessive absences were unusual, but she thought herself lucky that they hadn't fired her yet. She needed the internship. It was one step of her five-year plan, scrawled on yellowed paper and kept in her backpack. A constant reminder she unfolded to keep her on the right track. Law school, internships, job offers, happily ever after. So it was written, so it would be. Her magic promised her that. Ellie was an excellent student, a favorite among her teachers and bosses. She had never given them a reason before to question her dedication and work ethic, and so they were willing to let this mistake slide.

But not everyone at her internship was as forgiving. Violet Caldwell, for one, had been acting cold towards her since she got back. They were not close to begin with, but since Ellie's return, Violet distanced herself even more. Violet had tried in the past to invite Ellie to get to know the other interns and herself. Ellie, however, always turned down the invitations, preferring to spend the night with Derek. After a while, the invitations stopped coming.

Regardless of what Violet thought about her, they had to work together. Ellie wouldn't let a sour classmate ruin her chances of getting a good recommendation letter from the partners at the law firm. They sat together in a small office, if they could call it that, looking over research together in silence. Ellie preferred the silence, finding it easier to concentrate. After finally returning to her internship, things were back to normal, and Ellie craved normal more than anything else.

"I saw you the other day with a dude. Is that your boyfriend?" Violet asked, breaking the silence and Ellie's peace of mind.

"Uh... yeah, that's my boyfriend," Ellie's heart beat furiously in her chest. She wasn't sure why she was so nervous.

"How long have you guys been together?" Violet ruffled through the piles of research.

Ellie noticed she didn't look to be that interested in what she asked. She reasoned that engaging in small talk could thaw some of the ice between them. There was no reason to panic, yet.

"For almost three years."

Violet was quiet for a few moments, squinting at the paper in front of her. "Where did you meet him?"

"At a bar."

"Paradise?" asked Violet.

"No," Ellie's heart started beating faster against her ribs. "A different bar."

Violet didn't look up from her stack of papers, but Ellie watched her. Why would she ask about Paradise? Was Violet there on the day of his murder?

Violet turned towards Ellie, her face blank. "He seems nice," she said.

Ellie waited for her to say something else, but Violet got up and walked towards the copy machine.

"I'm going to give these to Scott," she said, and when the copies finished, she left the room.

Anxiety coursed through Ellie's body, and she struggled to keep her emotions in check. *It's a coincidence*, she told herself. *But how does Violet know about Paradise?* The worm in her brain now had a voice.

Ellie had trouble distinguishing her intuition from her anxiety. The sinking sensation of her stomach dropping like it did during turbulence. That was instinct. The achy heart and shaky hands were her telltale signs of anxiety. Her legs trembled beneath her desk, and her hands shook, and yet she felt so nauseous, she had no clue what to think.

Violet knew something, or perhaps Ellie just imagined it. She couldn't be sure, but when Violet came back into the room, she observed her more closely than she had before.

Violet brushed her black hair away from her face and looked at Ellie with her sleepy gray eyes. "Do I have something on my face?" Ellie looked away, embarrassed.

"No, I was wondering if Scott said anything to you about my absences." Scott Pruitt was one of the junior associates in the firm, and the one lawyer she worried would admonish her in front of the bosses.

"Please, as if that asshole knows the difference between any of the interns. I doubt he even noticed you weren't here for like a week." She plopped down in her chair and sighed. "I'm hungry. Do you want to come with me to grab some dinner?"

"I have to go home." Ellie lied.

"Back to the boyfriend?" The question sounded like an accusation. Ellie smiled, but she was sure her smile didn't reach her eyes.

Ellie came home to find the lights off and the apartment empty. She called out, expecting Derek to answer. He should have been home already. She dialed his number while checking every room in her small apartment, finding them all empty. The call went to his voicemail. When she called again, he still didn't answer. She found herself relieved to not find him. Something was wrong.

For months, Violet had never asked her anything personal about herself. When Ellie made it clear in the early days of their internship that she wasn't interested in being friends, Violet stopped pursuing it. Why ask her about her boyfriend now? Why did she mention Paradise? Unless she knew something about the night he was murdered.

Ellie walked into her closet and pulled down the box where she kept her few supplies. She hid it behind a box of mementos.

She didn't bother hiding it since she had told Derek the truth. If the police raided her home, they would find the contraband, but even Derek wasn't interested enough to snoop in her closet.

She was mundane; she liked it that way. It was how she survived. As far as people knew, she was a Mexican American girl from California, whose mother had died from cancer. She now lived in the Northeast for law school. There was nothing interesting about her. Police didn't raid random people's houses, but they did on tips from the public. She was safe as long as the facade fooled people.

She pulled out her mother's book. Before the resurrection spell, she hadn't touched the book since her mother's death. She remembered how it felt pulling it out the night of the resurrection. The book had an energy, a current beneath her fingers. A pulsing warmth that made the hair on her arms stand up. She flipped to the spell and pored over the contents. Everything she did that night was correct. She used the right ingredients and said the incantation right. It couldn't be a mistake in her working.

She tried to remember what his soul had felt like when it had passed through her body. Cold, like being dunked into an ice bath. Her breath had become stuck mid-gulp. She had nothing to compare it to. Is that not how all souls feel? Devoid of life, why wouldn't his soul feel as cold as his dead body?

She shut the book and put it away. She pushed the box back into the back of the closet. Something didn't sit right with Ellie, but he looked fine. He told her he was fine. But why did she feel off? The spell worked; she should leave it alone. Live happily ever after with the man of her dreams. There was Violet to contend with, but maybe she overthinked that, too. She was fine. Everything was okay.

Ellie spent the rest of the night trying to take care of herself. Eating whatever leftovers she could find and crawled into bed early. As she muttered, 'Everything is fine' over and over, it lulled her into a restless sleep.

Don't move.

A soft voice whispered urgently in her ear, waking her up. Her limbs weighed her down, and she tried to turn on her back.

Stop. Stay still.

Ellie listened to the voice, breathing as if she were still asleep. Her closed eyelids grew darker as someone blocked the streetlight from her window. She could sense someone standing over her. Their hand outstretched, wanting to touch her but stopping themselves. She wondered whether she was still dreaming. The nightmare found itself outside her head.

Her heart rate quickened. They lingered for far too long, and Ellie felt an itch on her arm, begging to be scratched. She stayed still, pretending to sleep and praying for them to leave.

The light shifted beneath her eyelids, and the familiar shuffling steps should have put her at ease, but her heart only beat faster against her ribs. Derek walked away from her. She heard him turn on the bathroom lights and close the door.

Chapter Five

Ellie arrived at school early. The law building was empty since most people were still in class. The heat from the building warmed her hands, and she pressed them onto her cold face, reddened by the strong September wind. Her hands raked through her windswept hair. She settled onto one of the black couches by the windows. A sense of ease and calm settled in her at school.

Her home had become a lab. Derek, the unsuspecting subject. She measured every moment, movement, and off-reply, and tried to measure it against what had been their normal. Did an eye roll strike her as odd or menacing? Derek's scoffing at something she said wasn't out of the ordinary, but did it sound harsher now? Meaner? She barely had a moment to rest when anything he said or did would need to be compared to their past. Away from home and Derek, she had nothing to do.

She pulled out her textbook since she had time to kill. Her eyes didn't register any of the words. Although she tried to concentrate, her mind unwillingly wandered to the night before. The images played out like marionettes controlled by an unknowable hand.

She sat in the audience, outside of her body, and watched as Derek stood over her, his hand outstretched. Something about the figure frightened her. Derek's face betrayed nothing.

She remembered the voice telling her not to move. She thought she had imagined it. The urgency in the voice made Ellie follow its instructions. She didn't normally hear disembodied voices, and she had never seen a ghost, but she didn't know what else could have whispered in her ear.

She brought the textbook closer to her face, pushing the confusion away. Perhaps it wasn't supposed to be sinister? Her eyes were closed after all, but what teetered her thoughts was how her body tensed under his gaze. How her heart pounded against her ribs, and her breathing slowed so as not to make noise. Like being frozen in place, staring at a rattlesnake, warning her of its strike.

"Hi, sorry. Do you know what time it is?" A deep voice snapped her out of her memory.

She looked up at the voice. A man stood in front of her. He had curly dark hair that looked reddish in the setting light. His eyes appeared golden in the light, but as he moved his hand to block the light from the window, she realized they were a lovely light brown. He waited and Ellie cleared her throat.

"It's 4:29," she said, looking at her phone.

"Oh, I have some time then," he said, sitting next to her on the couch.

Ellie peered down at her textbook. The words slipped through her mind as she read through them. The man's cologne fanned towards her. A strange fruit she didn't recognize. There was something else — an almost sterile smell. It reminded her of lonely nights spent at the hospital, watching the news in her mother's room. Numb to the outside world, as hers fell apart.

"What are you reading?" he asked.

She pulled the cover of her evidence textbook for him to read.

"You're a law student," he said.

"What do you study?" she asked, trying to be polite. This close to him, the man looked older than her. She liked the laugh lines lightly etched on his face. A few premature gray hairs stood out against his dark, wavy hair. She didn't want to talk. She'd been looking forward to having a moment to herself, but even away from Derek, her mind brought him everywhere.

"I'm not a student. I teach a class here," he said.

"What on?"

"Forensic Anthropology."

"Oh, I didn't know that was a class."

"It's a field of study. I just teach an entry-level course for master's students."

"So, you know about bones?" she asked.

"Yeah," he laughed. "I know quite a lot about bones." He had a brilliant smile. It reached his eyes, crinkling them.

Ellie smiled too, feeling a warmth flush through her body. She looked away, hoping he wouldn't notice the blush coloring her cheeks.

"I'm sure it's a lot more interesting than law," she joked.

"Oh, I'm not sure about that. My clients are not as chatty. I'm sure once you work as a lawyer, you'll be told all sorts of scandalous stories."

"Can't you tell if a person had a scandalous life based on their bones?"

"I can tell a lot of things through bones, but whether a person was interesting, I'm afraid not. The human body keeps a record. I can tell what a person ate, and how they maintained their body. I can tell how tall they would have been. How many times they broke a specific bone, and how the medical practices of the era mended it. How long they lived and even who their family was. But stories, I can't get that from bones."

"You seem to get quite a bit."

"Not enough for me, I guess."

"What are the oldest bones you've ever worked on?"

"Hmm," he scratched the top of his head. His eyes had a tenderness to them, and his fingers looked steady. Hands that were used to holding the most delicate objects in a firm yet gentle grasp. "I think the oldest was when I was in grad school. It was a femur and a few parts of the pelvic girdle. They were around three thousand years old. They found them in a cave in Iraq. I spent hours in the lab with them. You speak of stories, but when I worked in the anthropology lab, I would often wonder about the stories that hid in all the artifacts. I wanted to know everything about those people."

Ellie perked up at the mention of the topic. "I once saw a picture of a cave painting. There were these squiggly lines on a cave ceiling. They were small, and researchers were trying to figure out how they painted the lines. The people wouldn't have been tall enough to reach the ceiling. I guess they found their bones and figured out they weren't that tall. But do you know what they discovered?" she asked.

"What?" His gaze held hers, and Ellie couldn't look away.

"They were the finger paintings of children. Around three or four years old. Parents were lifting their children up to paint the cave ceiling. They had them hoisted up on their shoulders, and the children would drag their fingers over the rock, leaving their marks." Her own hands reached up, scraping an imaginary ceiling.

"They were human," he said.

"Yes. The first time I read that study, I cried. It's so silly."

"It's not silly."

"I guess the idea that parents in ancient times were just as concerned with letting their children play and create art, and not just focused on survival. I don't know, it made me feel like they were real, if that makes sense."

"They were not so different from us."

"Exactly."

"Are you interested in anthropology? Maybe you should have looked into it."

"I used to have an interest in anthropology in undergrad. But I guess I needed a career where I felt like I could actually make a decent living."

"I mean, academia isn't bad."

"But you're not an academic?"

"I'm not. Fair point."

"And anyway, I want to be a lawyer. My mom and I used to talk about my future a lot when I was a kid. She was really into education, and I was good at school, but I wasn't so interested in being in school forever. She wanted me to be a doctor. But I told her it took too long, and it was too much school. So, I asked her what took the least amount of time of all the careers she wanted for me, and she said, a lawyer. If I'm honest, if she had persisted with the whole doctor thing, I probably would have become a doctor. But she supported my decision to be a lawyer," she said. The image of her mother's smile when she graduated high school played in her head. She had been so proud, so happy. She had died before she graduated from undergrad. Ellie hadn't bothered walking in the ceremony.

"Will she support you if you decide to change your mind?" he asked.

"I'm sure she would have."

"I'm sorry. I probably shouldn't ask. But you seem so sad when you talk about her. Did—"

"She passed away a few years ago," she interrupted, not letting him finish the question she was used to hearing. She wanted to stop the sting that immediately followed the 'What happened to your mom' question.

"I'm sorry to hear that." He looked sincere about it too.

Death was a funny thing. Ellie had grown accustomed to the half-whispered 'I'm sorry' over the years. The awkward people who didn't know what else to say. The people who had their own complicated feelings about grief, and who were too afraid to examine death too closely. Then there were the genuine ones, people who understood. Ellie never understood why there were such few of them. Hadn't everyone lost somebody? Ellie had gone to the funerals of her great-grandmother, her grandmother, and finally her mother's. Death was constant, much more than life. Yet the people she could engage with, the people who had experienced losing someone, seemed few.

The stranger had lost someone. She could tell from the way he looked at her. Not with pity, or sadness, but with familiarity.

"What's your name?" she asked.

"River Mathews." He reached out his hand to shake hers. She giggled, thinking it a rather formal gesture, but reached out too. He held her hand longer than she thought normal, but she hesitated letting go herself.

She was about to introduce herself when she noticed his silver watch glinting in the late sun's rays. She was about to ask him about it when someone took her attention away.

"Hey," she heard.

She turned to see Violet standing near them, her hands on her hips. Ellie didn't understand her look. Was it accusatory? Bemused? But Ellie let go of River's hand as if it burned.

"Class starts in like a minute. You coming?" asked Violet.

"Yeah," said Ellie, flustered, trying to shove her thick textbook back into her backpack. She stood up fast, and River did the same. She turned to look at him. He waited for something, but she didn't know what. She smiled, not bothering to say goodbye, and walked away with Violet.

Her ears rang as she sat in class. She noticed her heart beating hard against her chest. The gnawing sensation in her stomach started again, and the memories of the previous night with Derek came flooding back. Where had all those feelings gone in the past half-hour?

"Hey, are you listening?" Ellie turned towards Violet. She sat next to her, which was odd. Normally, Violet sat at the back of class.

"Sorry, what were you saying?"

"I was saying, did you get the email from Professor Bennett about tomorrow's class?"

"No, I must have missed it."

"He's canceling class. Since we have a test next week for this class, I was wondering if you wanted to study with me tomorrow?"

"No, sorry. I have something I need to do." Ellie lied.

"Okay," said Violet, but something in her tone made Ellie uneasy.

Ellie opened her mouth to speak, wanting to elaborate on her lie to not hurt Violet's feelings, but her professor walked in.

She tried to concentrate, putting not only the previous night's thoughts away but her afternoon with River as well. But her mind had other plans.

Ellie realized why she hadn't wanted to let go of his hand. For the first time in weeks, she experienced a sense of peace. *How strange*, she thought, *to find peace with a stranger.* But she had seen his watch on his wrist. Maybe it didn't work, but Ellie had a sneaking suspicion he just needed an excuse to talk to her.

Her professor lectured on, but Ellie thought of River. Of his cheerful smile and warm eyes. Of the heat that spread in her chest when he looked at her. She would have continued to think of him. She would even have constructed elaborate fantasies in her head about him. If it hadn't been for the wriggling thought in her brain.

Derek.

Chapter Six

For the rest of the night, River felt stupid. He lay in bed, his eyes glued to his bedroom ceiling, cursing himself. He had been with her, talked to her, and he didn't even get her name. Even her classmate hadn't called her name. He had been so close and failed. He didn't dare breathe a word about the animated corpse he'd seen in the car with her.

His warning would have scared her. River thought he had more time to ease her into the truth. He knew from experience that you didn't spring bad news on someone. It was a delicate procedure, so if he wanted her to take his warning seriously, he had to gain her trust.

River groaned, lying on his side, staring at his phone. He thought of looking through the class directory on the school's website. He had found out one vital piece of information. She was a law student, which narrowed the search. But after a quick investigation, he found he didn't have access to the law school students' names.

He thought he was back at square one, but he reminded himself he wasn't. She spoke to him, and he'd been with her. He had watched the small intricacies of her emotions as they played out on her face. *She's more beautiful in person*, he thought.

With soft brown hair that he wanted to touch, and full lips he wanted to kiss. River stopped himself. He couldn't think about that now. Not after he had failed so miserably to get her name. But watching her eyes grow sad as she spoke about her mother had had a strange effect on River. Who was this woman?

After he first saw her outside of the law building, River dreamed of the dead man's girlfriend every night. The dreams would often start at the parking lot, where the smell of exhaust lingered in the air as she kissed the dead man. Time slowed down, and her hair moved with the wind. He could see every individual hair, the goosebumps on her skin, and the dark circles under her eyes. Did he notice she was so tired the first time that he met her? He wasn't sure.

As the nights wore on, the dreams changed and grew more vivid. Some nights, they would talk outside the law building. The intensity of her gaze held him in place like an inescapable vise. He wanted to know so much about her, but getting information from her turned into quite a task.

After every question, she would bite her lip and then just ask questions about him. She would ask him about his life. It would all spill out, even the parts of himself that he thought he would never tell, but he didn't need to be guarded with her. Not while their meetings were confined to his dreams.

So, he told her about his gift. The times he used it for good, like when he saved his friend from his untimely death while playing on the train tracks. Also, the times he ignored it, like when her boyfriend died. She looked hurt when he told her that. Other times, he would lament about the important person he couldn't save, the one that haunted his life even now.

On other nights, his dreams would escalate into terror. There were dreams when he tried in vain to move from the spot in front of the science building, to save her from a falling crane. Or he would watch in horror as she would faint from nowhere and his feet sunk into the ground. The earth would swallow him up before he even said a word.

One night, however, River cradled her head in his lap. His fingers played with her hair. The dream was more intimate than the ones before it.

"You have a freckle on your nose," she said to him, her fingers lightly brushed it.

The smallest of touches made his skin pucker. He clutched her hand to kiss it, the small fingers curling in his palm. She wriggled her hand free from his grasp and lowered it to the bulge growing in his pants. River stiffened at her touch but relaxed as she unzipped his jeans.

His dreams devolved into fantasy pretty quickly. At first, he was ashamed of himself. Here was a woman who needed his help, and his dreams wanted nothing more than sex. After a while, and after a few dream-induced orgasms, the shame vanished.

Despite not knowing her name, his obsession with the mystery woman consumed River. He awoke from each dream with a sense of peace he didn't understand. She was important to him; that much he knew. Her impending death loomed over him, refusing to leave him alone. It left an emptiness in his chest, as if something had consumed his heart. His premonition crystallized; she would die, but his gift insisted she was meant to be in his life somehow. The conflicting messages left him confused.

In the morning, as he got ready for the day, the images of his dream still lingered in his mind. They were in bed. His t-shirt hung loosely on her body. He wouldn't let her stay in his t-shirt for long. His fingers toyed with the hem, pulling it towards her stomach. Yet, she didn't reciprocate his playfulness. She wouldn't even speak to him, and River worried he had upset her somehow. He tried to catch her attention, but her lovely brown eyes avoided his gaze. He kissed her open palm, and she pulled away her hand.

"Have I done something?" he asked, worry growing in his heart. His hands traveled up her legs, ending at her hips. He leaned his face close to hers, pleading for a kiss. She scowled, but she didn't push him away.

"Find me," she whined.

"I've been looking for you," he insisted, kissing her neck.

"Look harder!" She didn't pull away, but let herself sink into his embrace.

"I seek you out at school every time I'm there. God, I would beg for just another glimpse of you. I look for you in the street, at the grocery store, the coffee shops. Everywhere." His cock became harder with every kiss and grind against her.

"Approach me. I don't bite. I'll be waiting in the law building tomorrow." She ground her hips against him, and he almost didn't catch that as his fingers pulled her underwear towards her thighs. He cupped her sex in his palms. She sighed in his dreams, and he felt her warm wetness on his fingertips.

The alarm on his phone woke him up, and he almost threw it across the room. The dream version of the woman swam in his mind while he lay in bed. River's frustration grew. He hated not knowing anything about her. He hated not knowing why she was important to him.

River didn't always understand how his gift worked. Exposure to the authorities kept him away from exploring it, and yet he got the sense that this was different. He wanted to probe his gift and let it tell him more about her. Whoever this woman was, whatever he had felt about her upon seeing her, she was something to him. He could only guess from his dream what he wanted that something to be.

He got in the shower, attempting to move on from the dream and get on with his day, but the dream woman drifted back into his mind. His hands slipped down onto his cock, already erect from a dream left unfulfilled.

The dream had felt so real. Her skin was soft, so warm, so inviting. God, he wished she were in front of him. As he worked his cock, with the hot water falling over his back, her voice floated back to him.

She would be waiting for him. This was his chance, but he was apprehensive. What would he tell her? That her boyfriend had been dead a week ago, and she was in danger? He wouldn't listen to it if a stranger told him something like that. He worried he would freak out yet another person, like he had in his past.

None of that mattered now since he hadn't been able to so much as get her name. But he knew now where her class was on Wednesday evenings. He would make himself available. Be there when she was. He had to gain her trust. He had to warn her.

As noble and selfless as he imagined himself to be, he wanted something else too, but he wasn't ready to admit it to himself yet. He wanted to get to know her. He wanted to see her again. See her beautiful, full figure walk towards him. Watch her lovely eyes gaze into his. Her full lips kissing him.

Chapter Seven

Derek huffed into Ellie's ear as she studied. She shifted away, pulling her flashcards closer to her face. Her textbooks, notes, and flashcards covered the tiny kitchen table. She studied for her evidence test in the evening and tried her best to ignore Derek's sulking next to her, but the longer she stayed at the table, the more difficult it became.

The energy of the room changed as soon as he walked in. He gave her a terse kiss on her cheek and stormed away into their bedroom. She stopped her urge to ask him if he was okay or if something was wrong. Derek hated that. He often told her how overbearing she was. It irritated him if she questioned his mood or his day. Ellie didn't believe she asked constantly, but she'd learned her lesson.

"Isn't it enough?" he would ask. "Isn't it enough that I'm here? Why do you always ask me if I'm okay? Or if I'm mad or sad, or mad at you? I'm just here, Ellie. There is nothing else going on!"

That had been an ugly fight. He left in a snit, and Ellie cried for hours after, upset with herself for needing the reassurance. But something always felt wrong.

Was it so bad for her to want to know why he felt that way? But it was an intrusion into his head and into a part of his life that he didn't want her in. The idea should have stung. Weren't they supposed to be entangled in each other's lives? But she had to remind herself there were aspects of her life she couldn't let him into either.

She tried to push it all aside when the thud of his angry footsteps grew louder as he came out of their bedroom. She read over the lecture notes from the previous week, ignoring the chair scraping across the wood floor as he shoved it back.

Her notes made little sense to her, and she cursed herself for not paying attention. During her last class, her mind had been elsewhere, wrapped around a man she had only met for a few minutes. How stupid could she be? She would never see River Mathews again, and now her grade would drop because of her little afternoon obsession with him.

After a few weeks of chaos, Ellie's life had finally slowed down. She had time to finish her work from school and her internship. She worked feverishly, getting ahead in most of her classes, her head filled with worry over the next unexpected event. Not that she wanted to jinx it, but whenever her life became too quiet, something always came in to shatter it. She thought she had more time, but when Derek sauntered in, she realized time had run out.

"What, you're ignoring me now?" he asked.

Ellie's heart sank. She measured her options: engage or not engage. The choice weighed heavily, knowing that either choice wouldn't end well for her.

"Sorry, it's just that I have a test in a few hours and I'm trying to study."

"So, your schoolwork is more important than me?" His eyebrows drew so close together they almost became one.

"Of course not, but you hate it when I ask you what's wrong," she said, defending herself.

"Yeah, because you always ask me when I'm fine. This is different. I'm upset."

She wanted to argue. Remind him of all the times they had had this fight before. Argue that he could put it aside for one afternoon for her sake. But she held back. It would only make things worse.

"What's wrong?" She asked instead, hoping for a small mercy.

"No, I won't tell you. Not when I have to beg you to have some sympathy from you."

"Derek, I want to know."

"It doesn't matter," he huffed, raking his fingers through his hair. "You can be really stupid sometimes, Ellie."

Ellie's eyes welled with tears, but she couldn't let herself fall apart. Not now, not before her test. She stood up, gathering her books and notes and shoving them in her backpack. Derek watched her, silent, his eyes following her every move, and a smirk creeping through the corners of his mouth.

Ellie left without a backward glance. She drove to school in a rush, wanting nothing more than to put as much space between her and Derek. She wanted to cry, but she stopped herself. It wouldn't fix things if she sat and wallowed, but her tears pooled anyway. She had a few hours now, and she needed to use them to study for her test.

Derek's angry voice replayed in her head. It wasn't even a new fight; that was what upset Ellie the most. They had fought about this countless times before. Why did he have to do it now? Especially when he knew she had a test later that evening and knew how important this degree was to her.

She walked into the law building, finding the same black couch empty. She settled in, taking out her notes to review. It worked for a little while, the anxiety of her evidence test keeping her on task, but Derek would wander back into her mind. The hot tears filled her eyes again. She reminded herself that the Derek problem would still be there after her test.

A gentle voice pulled her away from her thoughts. "Hello again."

She looked up to see River standing in front of her. He wore a green sweater; the sleeves rolled up, giving Ellie a peek at his toned arms. He looked happy to see her, his smile reaching his eyes. Almost relieved, although she didn't understand why.

After their initial meeting, she spent her evening ruminating about him. Their meeting replayed in her mind, remembering the warmth in his eyes and the calm she experienced that afternoon. She wanted to learn more about him and went to bed, telling herself she would search him up in the morning.

However, the following morning, as Derek kissed her goodbye and said, 'I love you' as he headed to work, her guilt slithered in her conscience. Why was she thinking about another man? She had a man. She brought him back to life! Why give River Mathews any more energy? She scratched out the idea of looking him up online after that. She didn't need to know him. He was a stranger, and the likelihood that she would see him again was low. Or so she imagined.

"Hello," she said.

He sat down next to her and whistled as he noticed her notes and books. "Test?" he asked

"Yeah, a huge one," she sighed.

"Maybe I shouldn't have interrupted you," he said.

"No, it's okay. I'm kind of glad you did. I don't think cramming is going to help much anymore." Ellie closed one of her textbooks with a decided thud.

"It might. I once studied for an hour right before my Russian history class in college."

"Did you pass the test?" she asked.

"Just barely. I passed the class by one point." He said, and he looked proud of himself too.

Ellie laughed. Goddess, it felt good to laugh. When was the last time she laughed? She couldn't remember. "Why did you take Russian history?" she asked.

"I needed an elective, and it was the only class available," he shrugged. He shifted in his seat, and she fell a little closer to him. She straightened up, her cheeks reddening. She shuffled her notecards in her hands, contemplating studying again, but she wanted to talk to River more. Guilt mingled with excitement as she threw her notecards into her backpack.

"Are you okay?" asked River.

"Yeah, I'm fine," she lied.

"Are you worried about the test?" he asked.

"Yeah," she lied again. She couldn't tell him about Derek. Opening up to strangers about her relationship issues was one surefire way to alienate them. Also, if she talked about her fight with Derek, she didn't trust herself to not burst out into tears. "I just want to do well on the test."

"You will," he said. "You seem like the studious type."

"You can say type A."

"I was going to say nerd, but I don't know you like that."

She giggled despite herself. "And here I thought I liked you."

"So, you're saying I already fucked up my chances?"

Derek flashed in her mind, but she didn't want to think of him anymore. Exhausted by always putting his needs and wants above her own, and angered by the fight, she wanted to be a little reckless.

"I wouldn't say that. You're lucky you can make me laugh."

"Well, at least I have something going for me then." He pulled her textbook towards him. "So, do you need some help to cram?"

"As helpful as your little story about cramming was, I think the time to study is over."

"You'll pass, don't worry," he insisted.

"I just really need this to work out for me," her voice caught, and she took a steadying breath to keep from crying.

"It will," he said, his tone much more serious.

"I wish I was as hopeful as you."

"You're not?" he asked. He gazed at her so intensely, Ellie had to look away.

"I am hopeful sometimes. But if I'm honest, I try not to be."

"Why?"

"Hope leads to expectations. And expectations have a way of being disappointing. Don't you think?"

"Not if expectations are realistic?"

"I guess that's my issue. I don't have realistic expectations."

"Well, there are realistic expectations and dreams. Dreams don't have to be realistic."

"They don't?"

"Not for me. I think it's okay to have wild dreams. I let them be as unrealistic as possible. That way, if even one percent of it comes true, it'll feel like a miracle."

"Do your dreams often come true even a little?" she asked. His cheeks colored red, and he looked away from her, flustered. She couldn't help but smile at his reaction.

"Well, some of my dreams come true. But if I'm honest, I wish more of them would." He turned towards her again, and he had the same look on his face, an embarrassed earnestness. This man liked her. She was sure of it now.

The blush spread to his neck. She saw it then, deep in the valley of her mind, an image distorted by fuzz. His lips pressed against hers, urgent and hungry. His fingers raked through her hair, grasping her nape as he kissed down her neck. She wanted to stay watching it; the premonition escaping like water through her hands. Leaving nothing but the remnants of a dream, she wished to fall into.

She told herself she needed to tell him she had a boyfriend. A man she loved. A man she sacrificed everything for. But she didn't tell River any of it. The premonition left her hollow, as if it had stripped away something precious from her.

"Have your dreams come true?" he asked, bringing her back.

"A few. I got into law school. I took a trip to Mexico and got to meet some of my extended family and explore the city from where my family is from. That had always been a dream of my mother's, too. She wanted me to see where she had grown up and where she had attended school. I had a personalized tour from my aunts, and they showed me all those places. As well as some places I doubt my mother would have told me about. Like the park where my grandparents caught her making out with her boyfriend. She wanted to go back more often than we could afford."

"But you made her dream come true. Even if she wasn't able to see it."

"I like to think so. Throughout the whole trip, I kept imagining what she would tell me. What jokes she would make about her home and the neighborhoods she used to play in. I thought I would feel her there. Like some part of her was still lingering there. It was a bittersweet dream to fulfill. But I'm glad I did."

River said nothing, but his eyes were warm with understanding. He recognized the pain and sadness that Ellie had experienced on her trip. It struck Ellie yet again how a stranger offered her more compassion than her own boyfriend. She never told Derek about the trip. She feared being ridiculed for looking for ghosts.

"What about you?" asked Ellie, trying to steer the conversation away from her pain. "What dreams are you waiting for?"

"I'm still waiting for the major dream of my life to come true."

"Which is?"

River licked his lips. Apprehensive about telling a stranger about his dreams. But were they strangers anymore? Ellie didn't feel like they were.

"I want to... it's stupid."

"No, please tell me." She reached out, placing her hand on his. He blushed again, but she didn't move her hand.

"I want to be known fully," he admitted. "It's silly."

"Are there parts of yourself you have to hide?" she asked.

"Don't we all?"

"Well, there are people who know us completely. At least in theory," said Ellie.

"Yes, but are there people who know everything about you? That you hide nothing from because you know that regardless of what you tell them, they'll still love you?"

"I used to have that person."

"Your mom?"

"Yeah." Ellie looked down at her brown loafers. River shifted, and his finger brushed beneath her chin. With the lightest of pressure, he guided her back to face him. Ellie didn't look away now. She didn't want to. There was so much kindness in those eyes, and even though she tried not to, she compared them to Derek's cold eyes earlier.

"You were lucky to have had her in your life. That she accepted all of you. I envy it. You'll find it again one day."

"We both will," said Ellie.

River wiped away a tear as it fell down her cheek. Ellie glanced down at River's lips and met his eyes again. Her blood rushed to her face, and she grew hot beneath his gaze. She pulled back a little, her heart racing. River pulled his hands away, a small cough breaking the spell.

Was she insane? She was about to kiss a stranger! River sat awkwardly next to her. The weirdness between them grew, and she tried to diffuse the situation.

"And here I thought you would have career dreams," she laughed, but it sounded forced to her ears. River laughed anyway.

"I don't have career dreams. Who dreams of labor?" he shrugged, laughing.

"What do you do, River?" It felt like a safer question to ask.

"What do you mean?"

"For work?"

"I…" he hesitated, "I'm a medical examiner."

Ellie's stomach dropped.

Chapter Eight

River knew he'd made a mistake. Ellie's eyes grew wide, a myriad of emotions playing on her face, landing on fear. He fought the urge to reach out and hold her. His chest hurt when he imagined her recoiling from his touch. Her face betrayed her feelings, and her panic was palpable.

"I have to go," she said. She started grabbing her things in a rush, her notes spilling around her.

"Wait," River reached out, grabbing her by the wrist. Mistake number two. Her eyes widened with fear, her body tensing at his touch.

"Let go of me," she said. Her voice warbled, but her gaze grew angry.

He wouldn't let her go. Not yet, not until he explained himself. She wriggled her wrist anyway, trying to escape his grasp, but he tightened his grip.

"Listen, I just want to talk," he started. He tried to make his voice sound even, not to freak her out further, but it didn't work. She grunted as she pulled her wrist back harder. If he let go, she would fall.

"Let me go," she said.

He pulled her in closer. Her chest and face by his. Her breathing came in shallow, panicked waves. He was scaring her, and he hated himself for it.

"You're in danger." River made his third mistake, but she stopped fighting him. Whatever plan he had flew out; he needed to be honest with her now regardless of the consequences. "That man you were with a couple of weeks ago — he's dangerous. I saw you come out of his car in front of this building." He saw much more that disturbed him, but he wasn't about to mention it.

"He was dead a few weeks ago. I know because I was examining his body at the morgue. You're in danger if you stay with him. I'm not sure what's going on or how he walked out of the morgue alive, but something's not right."

They stared at each other. He kept waiting for her to say something. To argue with him, or tell him he was mistaken, or crazy — but she didn't say a word. He let go of her wrist, forgetting that he had been holding it. His grip had been so tight, he left behind pale fingerprints on her brown skin. She didn't run, but she said nothing either. This close to her, he realized her dark eyes reminded him of an obsidian stone. He could see himself in them. Her lips were bow-shaped. He wanted to lean in and brush them with his finger, but whatever self-restraint he had worked in overdrive to keep him focused.

"Look." He reached into his back pocket, pulling out a card. "This is my number. If anything happens, or you need help, call me."

"You don't know anything about me. You know nothing about my life. I'm fine." She took the card anyway, but didn't so much as glance at it.

"Your name is Ellie." It came from nowhere, but River knew it was as true as his name. Saying her name seemed to snap her out of her trance. He couldn't be sure what he read in her eyes. Was she scared of him now, the way so many others had been in the past? Would she even believe him? He prayed she did. He prayed the past would not repeat itself. That he could at least save her.

Ellie turned away from him. He expected her to run, but she didn't. She walked slowly away, leaving behind a scent of vanilla and cedar that lingered around River. He fought every urge to run after her.

Chapter Nine

Ellie drove home carelessly after her test, her knuckles white as she gripped the steering wheel. She took the test in a daze, her mind fogging after every word. She was sure she'd failed. Each tick of the clock on the wall made her panic. No matter how hard she tried, her mind could only focus on River.

Whoever he was, he knew too much. He may not have known about the resurrection, but he knew Derek was supposed to be dead. She parked her car and ran to her apartment, the urge to hide growing by the second. To her surprise, she found Derek gone. She was thankful for it, not wanting to fight with him again.

She pulled River's business card from her backpack, finding it next to an old piece of gum in its wrapper. River Mathews. His phone number and his title, medical examiner, displayed prominently. She wanted to tear it up, destroy it into tiny pieces and pretend she had never met him, but her fingers gripped the card. She shoved it back in her backpack instead.

Ellie hadn't thought this resurrection through. She didn't have time to debate the consequences. She had acted on impulse, ignoring the most important rule her mother had always instilled in her. Do not cast in fear, anger, or desperation. She tried to reason with herself that River didn't know as much as she feared. Yet she couldn't stop the insistent feeling that something was off. How did he know so much? How did he know her name? Just her luck to bump into the freaking medical examiner at school.

His warning alarmed her. *Of course, he would think that I'm in danger*, thought Ellie. *I would be too if I saw a dead man alive again.* But River didn't know the complete truth of the matter, or else he would have known Derek was her boyfriend. Still, Ellie wondered if River thought Derek was the witch. Able to escape death and come back to life on his own. If he was going to turn her in, he wouldn't be trying so hard to warn her. And yet, who was she to him, she wondered. Why would he go out of his way to warn her?

She reached for her phone, her nerves having somewhat steadied after pacing for an hour. She scrolled to Derek's number and dialed. The phone rang and rang, and she tapped her foot without realizing. Derek's voicemail played. His recorded voice was no comfort to her trembling body. She hung up and called again, but Derek didn't pick up. She wanted to cry. Loneliness budded in her chest. Wasn't bringing him back supposed to make this feeling stop?

Derek came home later in the evening, kissing Ellie as she read her textbook. She flinched as his lips touched hers. If he noticed, he didn't mention it. She tried to remember what the test questions were, and what she had answered. She must have answered a few questions right, but the more she read, the worse her anxiety became. It had been the worst day to take a test. Derek, for his part, seemed ready to forgive and forget about their fight, and she couldn't have been gladder for it.

"Did you call?" asked Derek.

"Yeah, it was nothing," she lied. Ellie decided that until it became a problem she could no longer avoid, there was no reason to involve Derek in it. Maybe she was overreacting, and Derek would tell her so anyway.

Derek didn't ask her how the test went, and while a part of her was a little hurt by it, she wondered if it was for the best. They needed to move on, and she didn't want to tell him the truth of her afternoon.

At dinner, she sat across from him. River consumed her every thought, and her food went untouched. She looked up from her plate and noticed Derek hadn't touched any of his food either. Perhaps the fight had affected him after all.

"Are you not hungry?" she asked.

"I haven't really been hungry lately," he said. He shrugged, not bothered by the revelation.

"What like at all?"

"No. I mean, I eat, but it's more of a habit than anything else. It's like I don't get hungry anymore." He looked at her expectantly, as if for confirmation that this was normal. When he saw her worried expression, his mood shifted. "What? Is that not okay?"

"I don't know."

"What do you mean you don't know?" His voice raised a little, making Ellie's hair stand on end.

"I mean, it's not like I practiced this spell before. I had no clue what was going to happen after I brought you back."

"So I was an experiment?"

"I wouldn't put it that way, but I didn't have another dead body to try it out on."

"Are you fucking kidding me?" His face reddened, and Ellie tried to make herself small.

She waited for Derek to say something else, but he didn't. He got up, throwing his untouched plate into the sink, shattering it.

CHAPTER TEN

E llie awoke later that night from a nightmare. Her eyes snapped open to darkness. Her breath came in quick and her body trembled. The images of the dream faded, but the fear stayed. A sharp, skipping heartbeat and terror flooding every sense.

She reached her hand out in the dark to the other side of the bed, but where she hoped to touch the skin of her lover, she found instead empty cold sheets. She shot up and stared at the empty, rumpled patch. After turning on the lamp, she saw the faint outline of his head on his pillow. But she hadn't even noticed him leave.

Her tears welled up again as she rose from the bed. She walked around her small apartment looking for him, but he was gone. As were his keys from the bowl next to the door.

Ellie walked back into her room and headed towards the closet. She pulled out the box that kept her mother's things and, after rifling through herb bottles and oils, she found what she wanted. Her mother's tarot deck. Ellie didn't read tarot for herself often; she didn't like to peek into the future. To her, it was better to walk through life ready to be surprised instead of constantly checking that she was going the right way. It also didn't help that one of the last times she had used the cards, they had predicted her mother's death.

She still had hope then. She thought the treatment would work. That this momentary setback meant nothing and that her mother would be with her for decades to come. That all came tumbling down when she checked the cards, Death and the Ten of Swords. She tried to reason with herself that it was a symbolic death. Death of the cancer, death of the situation, and a new beginning to follow with her mother still with her. But as her mother went through her treatment, and things got worse, the Death card and its imposing horseman trotted through her mind. Reminding her of the inevitable end.

She held the well-worn cards in her hands. She had never bothered to get her own deck, and she had no clue where someone would buy them now, as metaphysical stores had all shut down. Turning them in her hands, she debated whether this was another huge mistake. But Derek's absence hung in the air, and she had no one left to turn to. She wanted to cry upon realizing that. She was alone, her mother long gone, and it was now that she wished she had someone she could ask. The cards were her only lifeline.

She shuffled them and turned the first card over. The Three of Cups. She examined it, bewildered. Was Derek out partying right now? On a Wednesday? She shuffled again, and this time asked out loud: "Where is Derek?" She grabbed the first card and flipped over the Hanged Man. A state of limbo? She tried to remember what the Hanged Man's other meanings were, but nothing came to her. What had her mother told her? It wasn't so much about knowing the cards but feeling them. She needed to be open to any messages that came through, but the only thing she could sense was the emptiness of the silence in her apartment.

She started shuffling the cards again, trying out more specific phrases in her head, when a card jumped out, skittering a few inches away from her. The King of Pentacles. It was peculiar, but she closed her eyes and took a deep breath.

At first, nothing came to mind, but pressure built in her chest. The card wasn't about Derek. When she thought of Derek, the pressure on her chest became hot, almost burning her skin. But when she focused on the King of Pentacles, the pain disappeared. He felt sturdy. Two strong arms enveloped her, as if a ghost stood behind her, pressing his chest against her back. Her skin erupted in goosebumps as the phantom blew on her neck. She turned around, startled, but the emptiness behind her left her wanting.

"Who is the King of Pentacles to me?" she asked, shuffling the deck. She grabbed the first card off the top, the Two of Cups. She grabbed the next card on top, the Ten of Cups. Was she sure the King of Pentacles wasn't Derek?

She asked next, "Who is Derek?" She shuffled the deck again, grabbing the first card on the top, the Emperor in reverse.

Ellie looked at each card, noticing the lush greenery around the King of Pentacles, and the harsh stare of the Emperor. She wondered who the second man could be, and her mind floated to River. His face slowly revealed itself in her head, like someone unwrapping a gift. A sudden rush of adrenaline made her heart pound in her chest. It couldn't be him? It was too random, and yet how often had her mother told her that coincidences were often signs.

Ellie stared at the card, trying to figure out how to phrase her next question, when she heard shuffling footsteps from somewhere in the apartment. She threw the cards into the box without a second thought and put the box back in the closet. She walked out of her room, her footsteps as quiet as the apartment. The low light from the window didn't help her sight, but the room appeared empty. She turned back towards her bedroom when her breath caught as a pair of hands appeared in the dark, gripping her throat.

Ellie gasped, her nails digging into the hands. She tried to pull away, bending forward to throw the assailant off balance, but the hands tightened. Panic set in, her heart racing as she tried to turn to make out the face of her attacker. Seconds passed by, but it felt longer. She struggled, her strength fading fast. She tried gasping for air, but the grip narrowed her windpipe.

Suddenly, she heard an all too familiar laugh, punctuated by her frantic gasps. The hands around her neck eased off, and Derek stepped into the light of the moon. She stared at him, stunned, as his laughter filled the room. Ellie coughed as tears streamed down her face as she tried to get air back into her lungs.

"What is wrong with you?" she choked out. Her fingers curled protectively around her neck; her throat throbbed with pain at the light pressure.

"It was a joke. Stop being dramatic!" He leaned in, giving her a kiss on her forehead and wrapping his arms around her.

Everything in her screamed to push him off, to be mad, but she stood petrified in his arms. She felt trapped, and if she moved again, he would rip off her head in one clean move. He kissed down her neck, lingering over her pulse point.

"Did I scare you, baby?" he whispered.

She wanted to answer no, but she was stuck between shock and absolute terror.

"You always liked it when I choked you before," he laughed against her neck. "It drives you wild. Doesn't it?" His hands flowed down to her sides, and he pushed them beneath her shirt, cupping her breasts.

She couldn't respond. The familiarity of his touch wasn't enough. She couldn't breathe, even now. As his hands roamed, her eyesight blurred her surroundings. The darkness closed in around her mind, her own thoughts coming back fuzzy.

"Was it too much?" asked Derek, taking his hands away from her body. He turned her around to face him, amusement in his eyes. He smirked and kissed her forehead.

"Let's go to bed," said Derek.

Ellie assumed he meant to have sex, but he didn't. He led her to the room, letting her go to her side of the bed. He left for the bathroom, leaving her alone to collect herself.

Ellie sat on the edge of the bed; her heart was only now slowing down. She placed her hands beneath her to stop them from shaking, but they trembled of their own accord. Her mind was strangely blank. She wasn't in her body. She was somewhere else. Floating above the bed. Above their apartment. Somewhere between the earth and space.

Derek came back into the room. Ellie thought he might have understood he had gone too far because he didn't touch her again.

She waited for an apology. She needed him to acknowledge how much he scared her. For the fight earlier that day. For stressing her out before her test.

They never came.

Chapter Eleven

It had been two days since River had spoken to Ellie. Two days spent tossing and turning and sleeping less than four hours a night. And thirty minutes since he dozed off in his office. The moment replayed in an endless loop. Her dark brown hair had a reddish glow in the sunlight. Her perfume still lingered around him, infecting his every waking moment with her memory.

River kept hearing their conversation in his head. Well, the conversation he had. He wondered if there had been a better way to phrase his warning. But it would never be a normal conversation. It couldn't be. There would never be a pleasant or easy way to tell her.

River convinced himself he was fine. Everything was fine. He had warned her like he needed to. He would move on with his life. Forget her and her undead boyfriend. Yet he was unsatisfied with the outcome. There was more he had to do with her. Why else would his mind and dreams not move on?

As much as his mind obsessed over the last bit of the conversation, where it all went wrong, he also replayed the beginning.

Ellie had been a beautiful enigma. The dream versions of her were woefully transparent to the real living, breathing version of her. He'd only just started scratching the surface. What sadness filled her? She had an air of wisdom accompanied by an innocent stare, making her even more mysterious to him. River wanted nothing more than to meet her again and talk some more. He wanted to learn what her favorite music was, what she liked to cook for herself when she was sad, and how she liked to be made love to. He wanted to know more about her life. The few snippets she gave made him hungry for more.

But a new, unsettling fear crept through every thought. Did she report him to the police? After all, he gave her all his information. She looked shocked to be told that the man she was with had been dead for a few days. What would stop her from turning him in?

As he pulled up to the morgue the next day, he expected to find the police there again to question him. The days passed, and nobody showed up, not even Ellie. He thought for sure that by now he would have at least had a phone call from her.

River was impressed with himself for figuring out her name. The name drifted from nowhere, in the empty space between a thought and opening his mouth to speak. He was right. Her brows shot up, and he watched her pale. He hadn't figured out her last name yet, but he strained to come up with it.

This was all new to him. He had grown used to his gift giving him warnings, but it had never given him someone's name before. His gift had also never pulled him this strongly towards someone. Almost as if compelled forward, his body was restless unless she was near. He hoped that his gift would give him something else, like her address or where she was during the day, but controlling it in that way proved difficult.

When he left his home, his eyes darted everywhere, looking for her, hoping to see her again. Hoping that if he talked to her again and explained himself better, he could save her from her fate that drew closer. Yet, if she hadn't taken his previous warning well, there was no way she was going to take her impending death any better.

River had never paid such close attention to his gift. He had spent most of his life ignoring it, pretending it didn't exist. He remembered his mother telling him he was wrong when he told her that Grandma was going to die in two days. Nothing but a dream, she had insisted. A nightmare his brain had conjured up after watching a horror film. He could still see the terror in her eyes as she hung up the phone three days later.

She wouldn't say anything to him for the next week, choosing to stay as far away from him as possible. That hurt. What hurt more, however, was the realization at four years old that he would have to keep a part of himself as a secret forever. He learned that what was just known to him, those thoughts that seemed to float like dust specks into his consciousness, were horrifying to everyone else.

His mom spoke to him again, but she never spoke of his gift. She didn't have to because River never brought it up again. But he got used to her suspicious sideways glances and the silences after he spoke, as if she waited for more. The hushed whispers between his parents would intensify whenever River said something innocuous; they took everything as a premonition. His knowing became an unspoken secret hanging over them all. Every word from his mouth became an omen, and as much as River told himself he loved his parents, his gift impeded him from opening up to them. He pushed away the knowing, pretending to be the boring son his parents wanted him to be. But some things slipped out.

Throughout his childhood, there were events he needed to stop. He saved his friend from getting run over by a car. Telling him he should stay home sick because they were going to have a pop quiz. A lie, of course, but his friend was safe and alive. Last he checked, his friend just had his fifth kid. He helped his uncle pick lottery numbers, and now his uncle lived in the Caribbean with his aunt and cousins. Never needing to work a day in their lives again. His gift was not all bad, and he knew that. Yet he often wondered how much better he would be at discerning the messages if he didn't try so hard to shut out every thought as soon as it began.

Some thoughts were too strong; like with Ellie, he couldn't fight them. Others were foggy pieces of nothing. Trying to decipher the messages was like looking at a blurry image without glasses. The more he squinted and tried to see it, the less sense it made to him. There were people he had saved, and he tried to focus on those the most. Although sometimes at night, he was haunted by all those he couldn't save.

His mind liked to dwell on the few people he thought he could trust to accept the preternatural part of him. But he still reeled from the sharp sting of rejection and disappointment after his mother's reaction. A part of him ached during every long silence from his parents. He thought of Natalie, her ghostly visage swimming through his restless sleep. She could love him if only the gift weren't real. And so, it didn't exist until the day that it did.

It became dangerous to use his gift when the Witchcraft Exclusion Act passed. Psychics, who once had storefronts selling their services, were the first to be caught. Their powers were public, and a quick search revealed their advertisements online. They didn't have much of a trial, and most pleaded guilty. River wasn't sure whether he would categorize what he did as a 'psychic gift,' but it didn't matter either way. He may not speak to spirits of the deceased, he might not look into a crystal ball to read fortunes, but he knew things. Things that he had no reason to know and no way to explain to someone investigating him.

The trials became entertainment, all televised for people to tune in and gawk at. He watched a few, finding himself unable to turn off the TV. They were terrifying as witnesses came out of the woodwork to 'expose' neighbors, friends, enemies. River didn't think most people on trial were witches. But watching the trials, he realized his secret would remain locked away forever. Kept with the shadows and fears that threatened to slither away when he wasn't careful. Anything unexplained became fodder for hysteria.

River stretched and yawned, looking at his messy desk. He checked his watch and tried to remember the last time he had been conscious. He's slept two hours and counted himself lucky no one had walked in on him.

His back ached as he stretched. He was too tired to drive home, and he needed some caffeine to perk him up, at least enough to where he felt comfortable that he wouldn't crash. He strolled out of his office, the smell of coffee beckoning him towards Books & Beans.

The place had a warmth that comforted River as he walked in. Along the walls were shelves of books, bordered by dark wood floors that creaked with each step. The coffee shop operated as a library of sorts. People would take and bring books as they pleased. River rarely knew what books he would find within the dark wooden shelves, but he had found a few classics he loved. He also found a copy of Frankenstein a few months back. It surprised him to see it, since the state banned it because of its depiction of witchcraft. Reanimation of the dead to them was a spell, not science, as the book depicted.

Molly, the owner, waved at him when he came in. Molly was tall and striking, with curly brown hair framing her face like a halo. She had luminous dark skin that glowed even in the low lighting of the cafe. She was cleaning out the bagel drawer when River approached the counter.

"What can I do for you, River? You don't normally visit this late."

"It's been a day, and I need some of your magic coffee." He hoped to come off charming, but Molly scrutinized him with her penetrating stare. He looked down at the counter, examining some Fall Festival flyers as if they were the most interesting thing in the entire shop.

"What's wrong?" she asked.

The question took him aback. *I must look horrible*, he concluded. "I haven't been sleeping."

"Nightmares." It wasn't a question, and he wanted to refute her assertion.

"No, they're good dreams, mostly..." he trailed off, not wanting to talk about his sex dreams with Ellie. "I just can't seem to sleep more than a few hours a night, that's all."

He felt a small pull from deep in his abdomen, like a string pulling him forward. A comforting warmth bloomed in his chest when Molly looked at him. He resisted the urge to ignore his gift. The warmth in his chest was familiar. The same sensation occurred when he was around friends and family.

Molly turned around to make his drink, and River turned back. There was one other person there, a woman with long purple hair that reached her waist. Her headphones were on and she read a book from the shelves in the coffee shop.

He could trust Molly. Every part of him was telling him so. But perhaps it was the sleep deprivation making his gift faulty? He wanted to tell her, wanted to tell somebody, anybody. It ate away at his insides, gnawing at the soft gray matter of his brain. He ran his hands across his face in frustration, his stubble scratching his palms. When Molly turned around, coffee in hand, the words started spilling of their own accord. He barely had any sense of what came out.

"Have you ever seen a dead man come back to life?" he asked Molly.

"Like resuscitated?" she asked, taken aback.

"No, like... his body was stiff. It was cold. It was in a fridge for days. And before that, it was food for wildlife. And then you see him driving the next day. Alive."

"I don't understand." Molly held his coffee cup in her hands, but she didn't give it to him. She watched to see what he would say next.

"I'm not making any sense." He put his hands on his face.

"River, I think you're overworked, that's all."

River peered up at Molly and let out a weak chuckle. "I think I'm going crazy."

"I think you are too," said Molly.

River laughed harder. Molly didn't give him the cup, but threw the coffee away in the sink. She grabbed a fresh cup and started working on a different drink. He couldn't make out what she was making. She turned around and handed him the drink.

"Drink this. You'll feel better."

"What is this?" He tried to remove the lid, but she stopped him.

"Never mind what it is." She rested her hand atop his, and her eyes locked on his in an intense gaze. "You are going to drink this and go home. Then you are going to get into bed and go to sleep. Do you understand?"

River felt strange as the room blurred around him, and his body felt far away. Each limb and bone disconnected from one another. His nerves pulled apart, stretching like taffy. His body was everywhere and nowhere, huge like the room. He noticed his hands on the wall behind Molly. His legs by the door. His ears were by the purple-haired woman playing soft Spanish music in her headphones. River wanted to tell Molly something else, but his tongue wouldn't move in his mouth as it rested on the bookshelf.

"I've always liked you, River, but you need to not bring that here. Do you understand?"

His vision blurred more, and he couldn't make out her eyes now. He nodded, and his head scratched the rafters above him. He wasn't sure that she understood him. She lifted her hand and tipped the cup into his mouth.

The sensation was strange, like plunging into hot water fully clothed. Peace flooded his system. He wanted to stay in it forever.

The next morning, he stretched his arms over his head. He awoke to find his head empty; he hadn't dreamed. No dreams of him kissing, talking, saving, loving Ellie. While a part of him felt disappointed, another part was thankful for some actual rest when he slept.

As he gradually awoke from his sleep, he jolted upright in bed. He found himself over his duvet, still dressed. His shoes were still on. Did he not want to change into his pajamas?

Confused, he got out of bed, swaying a little. He walked into the living room; he saw his car keys hanging by the front door. His backpack lay unopened on the couch. He walked to the window and saw his car parked in the driveway. He had no clue how he had gotten home.

Chapter Twelve

Ellie rifled through the mountain of paperwork on her desk at her internship. Violet sat next to her, reading through the piles of research. Her slouched frame made the top of her head disappear under the boxes on their desk. For Ellie, working through her worry and sadness wasn't anything new. She had done it many times before, but today it proved more difficult to do so.

Sleep had evaded her over the past few nights. She relived the terror of Derek's hands squeezing her throat. Over and over, the fear was as sharp as the night it happened. Nothing helped to take the memory away. Everything acted as a reminder. The universe wouldn't let her push it away.

The morning after the choking incident, Derek went about his morning routine as if nothing had happened. She waited for him to say something, anything that showed a little remorse or regret, but he looked unperturbed as he ate his breakfast.

"Where did you go last night?" asked Ellie. She hoped her question would be well-received, her tone laced with worry and care.

"I went out for a walk." He grabbed the orange juice from the fridge, turning away from her.

"At four in the morning?"

Derek stood quietly for a moment, drinking the juice. Ellie wondered if it was granting him time to plan his response.

"Remember when I told you I don't feel hungry?" He waited for Ellie to nod her head before continuing. "Well, I don't feel tired anymore."

"What?"

"I mean, I just don't get sleepy. I lie in bed and I wait for it, but it never comes. Even if I close my eyes and try, I never sleep, so I was walking around the neighborhood bored out of my mind."

Derek waited for her to reply, but since she stood silent and dumbfounded, he continued. "Guess you weren't expecting that, either?"

"No, I wasn't."

Derek scoffed as he finished his juice and started grabbing his things to leave for work. "The thing is, Ellie, you've changed since you brought me back. You act like I'm a different person. I don't get it. Why did you bring me back if you weren't going to trust me anymore?"

Ellie wanted to argue. He didn't feel the same. There was something off, like the feeling of forgetting whether she had unplugged her straightener on the way to school. A squirming thought that wouldn't leave her alone. The sensation only grew stronger the longer Derek lived.

"I'm sorry. I know you didn't ask for this." She reached to touch his hand, but he pulled it away. It stung. It shouldn't have. She should have been mad, but she longed for that connection again. The reason she had sacrificed everything for. She feared that if it were gone, the regret of it all would be too much to bear. "You can't touch me either, can you?"

As if to prove her wrong, he grabbed her hand. His touch made her flinch. His hands were icy, as if he had just stuck them in the freezer.

"Are you disgusted by me?" she asked. "Because I'm a witch?"

"No, I'm grateful. I promise you that. I could never repay you for giving me a second chance at life."

His fingers traced her hand, and Ellie wished he would pull her in closer. She would forgive him for last night's incident, but she needed him to apologize. This was different. It couldn't be swept up along with the petty everyday fights. Forgotten and forgiven without even an acknowledgment of his horrible treatment of her. Yet Derek looked unaffected.

"Derek?" she asked. "Do you remember what happened to you?"

"What do you mean?"

"The night you died. Who killed you?"

"No, I don't remember," he said quickly, and dropped her hand. He lied; Ellie knew it.

"If you remember what happened, we could find your killer. We could go to the police."

"And tell them what? My witch girlfriend brought me back to life, and now I know who killed me?"

"We could make something up. There have been unsolved murders all over this town for the past two years. What if you were their next victim?"

"Well, I wasn't, so let's leave it."

"Derek—"

"I said LEAVE IT!" Derek turned towards her, his face inches from hers. Ellie didn't move, her body too petrified to even flinch. He pulled back, but kept his eyes locked on hers.

She knew the routine now. She would stay quiet, drop the conversation, move on from the fight, and smile like he hadn't scared her. Not today. She didn't want to drop this.

"Why were you at Paradise? The night you died, you told me you were working late."

"Ellie, leave it," he said through gritted teeth.

"No, Derek. Why were you at Paradise?"

"To get away from you," he spat.

Derek hadn't gotten over the fight. Over the next couple of days, he stayed away longer in the evenings and only came home to lie down next to her before bed. He left for work without saying a word to her, and Ellie worked in a trance. Her head spinning with stories to fill in the gaps in Derek's story. She tried not to let any of the past events impede her work, but her overthinking overpowered her will. She'd already misplaced two textbooks, a motion to appeal, and her laptop.

As she tried to organize the cover letters for the evidence, her mind returned to the argument. She didn't want to think about it. With skipped classes and sloppy work at her internship, she was sure her scholarship was in jeopardy. Although Derek had taken all her attention and energy over the past couple of weeks, she wanted to appear normal to everyone else.

Ellie found it hard, however, to act as if everything was normal. She wasn't in the clear with the police yet. The occlusion and protection spells she cast before rescuing Derek seemed to work. But anybody outside the police force could come in and read his file and discover their incompetence. She had been lucky that Derek had remained unidentified while he was dead, but she worried the police would find out Derek was the missing body. She would have to take care of that as well, but she had spells in her mother's book that could help erase minds if it came to that.

There was still River. She had waited with dread to see if he had told the police about her. But days passed by, and no police came to her door. Maybe she was safe there, too?

Although every bone in her body told her to investigate what happened to Derek, she was instead at her internship doing the grunt work. She wasn't alone, however, as Violet sat next to her, rifling through the same stack of papers. If she left now, Violet would tell the associates, it wouldn't look good. She wasn't willing to risk more than she already had.

"Hey, do you have the third page of the motion to appeal?" asked Violet. Her black hair was in two braids down her back, and she played with a small strand that framed her face.

"Yes, hold on," Ellie looked through her stack. "Wait, I think I left it by the copy machine."

Ellie placed the stack on her lap on the floor and walked over to the copy machine by the window. She enjoyed being at her internship again. Doing homework and going to class felt like activities from another life. Her classmates talked about publishing in journals, upcoming tests, and annoying professors. Their lives wrapped around their uncomplicated futures that Ellie craved.

She found the motion on the copy machine and then peered out the window. The fall winds pushed the yellowed leaves off their branches. How was life continuing like normal? It was almost comforting in a way. Life moved on, so would she and Derek. They would get used to this new version of themselves. The harsher, imperfect versions of every couple that creep out of manicured facades. Everything would go back to the way it was, eventually. She hoped for it.

She stayed by the window for a moment longer. Violet wasn't in a rush to get the paper. She stayed watching the leaves swirl. But then, something moved. A flash of black amongst the yellow leaves. It moved too fast. If she blinked, she was sure she would've missed it.

Then she saw it again; this time, it stayed stock still. Watching her. Standing next to the tree, a creature stared back at her. She had seen nothing like it before. Its face birdlike; it reminded her of a vulture. She discerned an almost humanlike body attached to the face, but it was larger than any person she had ever seen. Inky black feathers covered its body, and its iris-less eyes didn't move from her own. She gasped, dropping the paper on the floor.

"What is it? You can't find it?" Violet stood up and walked towards Ellie. She picked up the paper Ellie had dropped. "It's right here."

Ellie tried to block the window with her body, hoping that Violet wouldn't find it suspicious.

"What's going on?" asked Violet, craning her neck to peer beyond Ellie's shoulders.

"Nothing," said Ellie, bending towards the side Violet looked through.

"What?" she laughed. "What are you blocking?" Violet pushed her away from the window, and Ellie held her breath. Violet turned back towards Ellie, with a perplexed expression on her face. "What did you not want me to see? The leaves?"

Ellie didn't know what to say. Had she imagined the creature?

"It's a nice day," said Violet as she looked out the window again. Ellie did too. She scanned the area around the tree. The creature was gone. The red oak tree stood alone, and she watched as a couple of teenagers crushed its leaves underfoot as they walked by.

Relieved, Ellie turned to return to her desk when suddenly a flash of black passed by the window. She whipped her face back towards the window and recoiled as the creature pressed its birdlike face against the windowpane. Its breath fogged the window. Its beady eyes darted between Violet and her. Violet screamed and ran back to the window, yanking the blinds closed. She turned towards Ellie; her face was red and livid.

"That's it! What is that?" she asked Ellie.

"You can see it too?" Ellie said, not quite believing it, because it would make the creature real.

"Of course, I can see it! Did you not see it squish its ugly face on the window? What is that, Ellie?" She pulled Ellie away from the window. "I tried to be nice. I tried to ease my way into this, but time's up, Ellie. What did you do?"

"What?" Ellie's mind hadn't moved from the creature. She didn't register what Violet said.

"Your boyfriend is supposed to be dead! You know how I know that? I killed him."

"What?" Ellie's ears rang.

"It's a long story; actually, it's not. He tried to kill my friend! It was him or her, and trust me, he deserved what he got!"

"You killed him?" Ellie asked, the information sinking in.

"Yes, and you brought him back to life, didn't you?" She waited for Ellie to say something. To refute it or argue, but she didn't. There was nothing Ellie could say to get out of this now. "You're not supposed to bring people back from the dead!"

"You're not supposed to kill people!"

"It was to protect my friend. He almost killed and assaulted her. If I hadn't had a premonition that she was in danger, he would have killed her and moved onto his next victim."

"That's not true." Ellie shook her head, her anger building in her voice.

"Oh yeah? And you were there, right? At Paradise when he hit on my friend?"

"You're lying."

"You're lying to yourself. How well do you know him?"

"I've been with him for two years."

"And you know everything about him?"

"Of course I do."

"Really? So what was he doing the night I killed him?"

"He was at Paradise with his coworkers."

"That's a lie."

"It's not!"

"You don't know, do you? He's been lying to you about it, hasn't he?"

"He hasn't."

"You're lying," Violet almost laughed.

"You don't know anything about my relationship. You don't know me!"

"And whose fault is that? You never talk to anyone in class. Hell, we've been in this internship together for months and I'm lucky if you even say 'hi' to me."

Ellie wanted to explain herself. Tell Violet everything. Tell her that her mom died, and that she didn't have anyone else. Derek was it. She loved Derek. He had been there for her at her lowest. He held her in her sleep and kept her safe. She had to bring him back from the dead. He was all she had left. Ellie held on to him so tightly there could never be room for anyone else. She didn't mean to be rude. She didn't mean to ignore her or her other classmates. Derek took over everything in her life, and if she wanted to keep him, she had to make him her universe.

It all sounded so pathetic in her head.

"Listen," Violet's voice was gentler, "you're clearly in trouble. Let me help you. I'm part of a coven. We can help you fix this." Ellie knew what she meant by 'fixing the problem.' They would kill Derek again.

"You've done enough." Ellie got up and walked out of the room.

She grabbed her bag and headed to her car. She needed help, but not Violet's help, or her coven's help. Violet had caused this mess! She unlocked her car and looked around, half expecting the creature to jump onto the hood of her car. She had other avenues of help, and they didn't involve another person.

As she pulled out of the parking lot, she noticed Violet staring from the window. Ellie couldn't make out her face well. Was it a look of murderous rage? Anger? Remorse?

No, Ellie realized, pity.

CHAPTER THIRTEEN

River changed into his scrubs. The fabric ran down his chest and abdomen as he stretched his arms over his head. He was more alert than he had been all week, and as he walked into the examination room, he pushed away the unease that lingered in his mind. Brian was already there, unzipping another body bag.

Early in the morning, a search group had discovered two missing women's bodies in the woods. They were abducted and strangled on the same night. With two new bodies plus the five left over from the day before, River found himself with a very busy day. Yet as he worked, bagging up the organs of each woman and placing them into the empty cavity left behind, the previous night's events invaded his thoughts.

He couldn't remember how he had gotten home. He remembered leaving his work and walking... towards his car? Yes, he thought that was right. He went into his car, but why couldn't he remember the drive? *Well,* he reasoned, *I take the same route every day. Why would it stand out?*

Still, he'd never fallen asleep with all his clothes from the day. At least not during a normal workday. Even if he'd been tired, he would have at least taken off his shoes.

It was two in the afternoon by the time he decided to get some lunch. The backlog of bodies took much of his time, and the work did little to ease his mind. He felt like he had missed something. He wondered whether it had something to do with his gift, but that made little sense to him. During his work, he daydreamed, piecing together what wasn't there. He needed to move on from it, but like a word forgotten mid-sentence, it was going to bother him until he could remember it.

After an unsettling morning, he stopped by Books & Beans and grabbed a coffee and a sandwich for a late lunch. Molly hummed while filling his order, giving him a brilliant smile.

"Hi River, the usual?" she asked cheerily.

"Yeah, that would be great. Thanks."

She got busy. Something was off with her, but River tried not to focus on it. His morning had been confusing enough. He didn't need to know why Molly acted as if she had just won the lottery.

"How did you sleep?" she asked.

"Good, actually?" he said, confused by her sudden interest.

"That's good to hear," she said, handing him his order. She looked pleased with herself, and he felt awkward, as if missing an inside joke. He left a tip and left the coffee shop.

He relished the fresh air, away from the smell of decomposing bodies and the acrid scent of chemicals, as he walked back to his office. The wind picked up, swirling newly fallen leaves around the commercial square. River wanted to eat his lunch in peace, away from the office. While he had been lost in his thoughts all day, Brian had talked his ear off about his suspicions about the missing dead body. River placated him by agreeing with some of his outlandish theories, but he seriously doubted secret cults that worshipped aliens made much sense. He wanted some peace, and the gazebo in the square was perfect.

Another strong gust of wind blew, and River raised his arms to guard his face from flying dirt, accidentally dropping his phone. He sighed, throwing his head back, wondering how many more minor inconveniences were left in store for him today.

As he bent to pick it up, a small pull stirred in his chest. He paused, and as he leaned into the sensation, the small stir inflamed. Spreading like tendrils from his chest outwards to his extremities. He looked towards where his gift compelled and saw her.

Ellie ran out of the library across the street. She rushed down the stairs, her brown hair swirling around her face. River watched her, unsure of what to do. He wanted to approach her, but the last time had gone so poorly he didn't want to upset her again. She was frantically looking over her shoulder every so often. Her eyes searched the skies, the streets, and down every alley as she rushed. He glanced in the direction she was looking, but there were only a few people left. Most were already back at work after the lunch rush. He was unsure of what she was looking for. His hand drifted to his chest and his palm met a racing heart. A cold sweat made his hands clammy and his body cold. She was in trouble. He couldn't stand back anymore.

She didn't notice him at first until he stood right by her, too distracted by whatever preoccupied her mind. She stopped, startled at seeing him so close. River tried not to let her groan hurt him. He was the last person she wanted to see.

"Ellie—"

"Please, just leave me alone, okay? I don't know who you are, or how you know my name, but I don't want to talk to you!" She'd been crying, and River wanted to brush away the tears that threatened to spill over. Something was wrong, but he wasn't sure how he would ever convince her he was trustworthy. He kept walking alongside her anyway. He couldn't leave her alone, not like this.

"You're right, I don't know you. But I can tell you need help."

"River, I'm fine. I know you think Derek was dead. He wasn't. He never was. Everything is fine."

"Derek? That's his name?"

"River..."

"Listen, you have no reason to trust me. I get that. I would be scared too. But that man is going to get you killed. I know it."

"How? How are you so sure?"

They had reached the alleyway between Books & Beans and the flower shop next to it. He reached out to stop her, his fingers holding onto her arms. He wouldn't have been so bold before, but he was desperate. His hands held her in place in front of him. Her eyes were teary again, and River fought the urge to hug her.

"I can't explain it. I'm sorry. But you have to believe me."

Her gaze didn't soften. She fought the warning, fought him. God, she was stubborn. She would never listen to him. The realization made River's stomach drop.

He couldn't save her.

"Please," he begged. "Just believe me." Her eyes wandered from his. She wouldn't even look at him. Her eyes fixed on something behind him. A look of surprise and terror spread across her face, her brown eyes growing wide.

"What are you looking at?" he asked, turning around. Before his eyes could focus, something pushed him forward. He fell to the ground, pulling Ellie down with him. A tremendous gust of wind blew dirt, trash, and crisp fall leaves around him. He tried to pick himself up, but Ellie's hands gripped his shirt, holding him down.

"Don't move!" she yelled, but the noise of the wind drowned out her voice. He looked around him, but only leaves and trash swirled around them. What had knocked him over? He looked beneath him; Ellie's eyes focused on something above him. Her body crouched under his. Her nails digging into his arms. River looked behind him, following her gaze, but stopped as a searing pain exploded on his forearm. The wind stopped almost immediately, and when he looked at his forearm, there, against his torn blue shirt, were three long gashes.

He stared at his bloody shirt, confused; he tried to find the source of the gashes, expecting to find corrugated metal or hell even a tin can, but found only plastic trash and leaves strewn around them. River caught Ellie watching him, her eyes fixed on the bleeding gashes. The sticky blood trailed down his arm, and River's sleeve became soaked.

"We need to take care of that," she finally said.

He got up and extended his unharmed arm to her. She took it and pulled herself up.

"You should go to a hospital. You may need stitches." Ellie looked worried, and River twisted his arm to see the gashes better. He paled a little at seeing how much blood poured out.

"I don't think it's that bad," he lied.

"Don't act tough," she said.

"I'm not acting tough. I have medical supplies in my office. We can go there."

He waited to see if she would reject his invitation. Her apprehensive eyes darted around the square. River found yet again nothing. She finally turned to him and whispered a small okay. He directed the way.

"I'm sorry about your lunch," said Ellie as they walked to his office.

"I wasn't hungry anyway," he lied, seeing the remains of his sandwich on the concrete.

CHAPTER FOURTEEN

Ellie's heels clicked on the floor of the empty morgue. She followed River, pretending to peer curiously around her, as if she hadn't seen it all the night she stole Derek's body. The morgue looked less sinister under fluorescent lights. Something about the dark had made her hair stand on end, scared that any of the bodies would start moving on their own as she stitched up Derek's chest.

His office was new to her. She hadn't entered it the night she broke in. The small office contained an oak desk taking up a corner of the room, along with two smaller chairs situated around it. Filing cabinets lined the wall by the window, and a tall, skinny bookshelf on the opposite wall had binders and framed photos. He reached into the bottom drawer of the filing cabinet and pulled out a first aid kit. He twisted his arm to get a better view of the damage, but sighed after a moment.

"What is it?" asked Ellie.

"It's nothing. It's just this is the worst angle." He started unbuttoning his shirt, and Ellie quickly looked away.

What was she doing here? She shouldn't have followed him. She should have gone back home and tried to find information on the creatures from her mother's book since the library had been a bust. But one look at his arm and guilt made her follow him.

As he shuffled about in his office, she looked at anything and everything to keep herself from turning around. There was a license for his work and a degree from a university in Texas. She walked over to a bookcase, and among the binders she saw pictures of River with various people. Some were older than he was. Family, she guessed. One photo had a young woman who looked a lot like him. They had the same smile and nose. Another photo had River standing in his graduation robes with his parents and his sister. He and his father had the same dark hair and both towered over his mother. Another photograph showed River with another woman. She looked nothing like him, so probably not a sister. The way the woman squeezed her arms around his waist wasn't a sisterly kind of hold.

River cleared his throat, and Ellie turned towards him, finding him shirtless. Her eyes lingered on his chiseled and lean chest before snapping back to his eyes.

"Do you mind?" he held up the kit. "It's at a weird angle. I'm having a hard time reaching it."

Ellie blushed, finding it hard to snap out of her shyness. She reminded herself River was a stranger. A stranger who had saved her and used his body to protect her from the vulture. Not many strangers would do that. He held the first aid kit up for her, and her guilt gnawed away at her. He hadn't been able to see what had attacked them. Not all mortals could see magical creatures. He got hurt because of her.

He was stronger than she realized, his muscles well defined. She hadn't noticed before. At school, she had found herself too focused on his warm brown eyes to have paid attention to the rest of him. Not that she had any reason to look, she reminded herself. His chest and neck flushed red. She peered up, catching his gaze. Her staring had been a little too obvious. She wanted to giggle at that, but she held it in. The situation was awkward enough, and she didn't want to make it worse.

She positioned herself at his side and examined the wound. The gashes were about four inches long but were thankfully not that deep. The middle wound was the longest and deepest. She was no doctor, but it looked bad enough for stitches.

"Are you sure you don't want to go to a hospital?" she asked.

"I'm sure it's not that bad."

"It's pretty bad." The lacerations were long, and bits of flesh hung away from his arm.

"I've had worse paper cuts," he joked.

"It's not funny. You're going to bleed out. Or it can get infected."

"It'll get infected if you keep stalling," he said with a smirk.

"Fine," she said.

He handed her rubbing alcohol and some cotton balls. She focused on wiping the blood away first to see the injury better. Ellie grabbed a new cotton ball and soaked it in alcohol. Returning to the wound, she cleaned the injury itself. He sucked in air as the alcohol soaked into the wound.

Her fingers lightly grazed the skin outside the injury, and the air grew thick between them. River's arm tensed, exposing the veins beneath his skin. Ellie finished cleaning up and held his arm as she wrapped it up in a bandage.

She didn't want to let go. Touching him, tending to him, quieted her scattered and anxiety-riddled mind. A peace settled in her chest, and as much as she wanted to fight it, her exhausted body just wanted to sink into it. The world stilled, and the stillness felt exquisite.

She realized then that the calm she had felt after she talked to him at school wasn't a coincidence. For whatever reason, his presence was enough to make her world and the chaos in it stop, if only for a moment, but she would take that moment. She had so little left. She was so entrenched in the calm; she didn't even realize he stared at her. Her eyes met his for a moment, the warmth in them startling her.

"Are you okay?" asked River.

Ellie smiled. "Shouldn't I be asking you that question? I mean, you were just mauled."

"Mauled?" he asked.

"I mean, whatever did this," she blurted.

"It must have been some flying type of metal trash," said River. Ellie thought it made no sense, but it probably made more sense than a magical creature he couldn't see. "And anyway," said River, bringing the focus back on her, "you were upset when I bumped into you."

"It was a hard day at my internship today, that's all."

"You looked like you were running away from something."

"I wasn't." She couldn't think of what else to say.

"Why were you at the library?"

Ellie took a moment to answer, focusing instead on securing the gauze around his arm. Blood pooled on the other side of the bandage. She could tell him the truth. Tell him about the creature she had never heard of or seen before today. The creature didn't exist in her mother's book, nor had she ever seen anything like it described in stories. She was afraid to look online in case her internet was being watched. They had gotten a few people like that, people who were no doubt innocently looking up information on goblins, mythology, or lore. Whatever objectionable magical information they looked for would land them the next day in front of a judge. Ellie thought that by looking in the library she might find something, but someone had long since pulled every book off the shelves that referenced anything remotely magical.

"I was looking up something I needed for my internship. The law library didn't have it. I thought the library in town would."

"Did you find what you were looking for?"

"No." She finished wrapping his arm, but she didn't want to move from where she stood. Afraid the calm of the moment would leave when she did.

"I'm sorry about the whole dead man thing." River said. Ellie stilled. "I must have thought it was someone else. I'm sorry if I freaked you out." He waited for her to say something, but she didn't, so he continued. "I have dreams sometimes, and they're so vivid. I must have confused one with reality or something. I didn't mean to scare you." His eyes were soft, pleading for her to forgive him.

Ellie reached up again, her hands resting on his arm. His breath caught as if her touch were cold. For a moment, she wondered what it would be like to tell him the truth. To let it all go and not complicate her life further. He looked at her with such longing, his eyes wide, as if surprised she hadn't run away from him after the attack. Her hand traveled down to his wrist, and his breathing slowed. His eyes never moved from hers. River was mortal, and letting him into her world was about the most selfish thing she could do. Murderous vultures were just the beginning of the dangers in her world. He didn't need to know.

And yet, his eyes begged for an explanation. Calm rushed into her body as her hand lingered on his wrist. If she let go, she wouldn't be strong enough to tell him.

"You weren't dreaming. That man is my boyfriend, Derek. He was dead and... I brought him back to life." She watched him, trying to make out his answer before he said it.

"You... brought him back to life?"

"Yes."

"Are you safe?"

Ellie couldn't answer. The calm broke, and fear flooded her system again. Her chin started wobbling, and her vision blurred. "No," she admitted.

As she cried and her body shook, River stood up to hold her. His strong arms kept her up, lifting her when her knees gave out. Her toes scraped the floor as he held her to his height. Her fingers gripped his shoulders, her nails digging into his warm flesh. If it hurt him, he didn't complain. Calm poured into her body. Her breathing evened out, and her body stopped trembling. It surprised Ellie how quickly it worked.

She couldn't understand it. How could she feel so safe and so at home in a stranger's arms? And why had she never felt this way with Derek?

"You can stay with me," River said.

"You don't know me," she protested. Her ear pressed against his chest, and his heartbeat matched hers. Slow and steady. Was her presence enough to calm him, too?

"Remember those dreams I told you about?" asked River. Ellie nodded, feeling a little more stable as he lowered her down. She looked up at him as he brushed her hair away from her face.

"You've been in my dreams. Every night since the day I saw you get out of that car. I didn't understand why I kept seeing you in my dreams. I didn't know what it meant. But I think I know now. Stay with me," he whispered. His voice sounded pained, and Ellie wanted to do what he asked.

For a moment, she could picture it. His arms around her, holding her tight, keeping her safe. He wouldn't choke her out of the blue. He wouldn't tell her she was being dramatic when she worried. River reached out, his hand cupping her face. Why did she get the feeling that he could tell what she was thinking? His touch burned through her, and her heart rate slowed. Her breath became shallow, and an achy feeling blossomed between her legs.

"I don't want to drag you into my mess," she whispered back, and he pushed her back against his desk. Her tailbone hit the desk before she sat on it. River pushed legs open, and he settled between them.

"But what if I want you to?" His voice was harsh against her ear; it sent shivers through her body. His hand drifted up her thigh. Her breath caught, but she fought with herself, wanting both to push him away and bring him closer.

"Let me in," he whispered, as his lips kissed her jaw. Ellie had enough. She pulled his face to hers and kissed him.

He kissed her hard, with an urgency and hunger expressed through his lips. Her need made her pull him closer. His hands squeezed her thighs before moving under her shirt. His fingers grazed beneath her bra, and Ellie swore her skin burned where he touched.

She wasn't sure what this was. How could she want someone she didn't even know? Yet, it felt so right. Instinctively so, every touch from River made Ellie's body respond. His light nip of her lips made her gasp. The pressure of his lips on her neck made her body buck into his hips. He pressed himself closer to her, and he groaned when she ground her hips against him. His voice broke her out of her haze for a moment.

Even if he wanted to be brought into her life, she didn't want to endanger his life. She couldn't explain it, but she cared too much about this, about him, to do that. She pulled away for a moment, looking into his warm eyes. There was a hint of red in his brown hair and in his beard, and she smiled, but it didn't reach her eyes.

In another life, maybe, she thought.

River noticed the change in her mood, and it looked like he wanted to say something, but Ellie wouldn't let him. She kissed him again, and he fell right into it. His hands moved, pulling her in closer, his chest flushed to hers. Ellie knew the spell by heart, having used it a few times before. She pulled away and pressed her forehead to his.

"Your mind wiped clean,

It's a brand-new day.

Your memories are gone

And you'll have nothing to say."

The heat bloomed in her hands almost instantly. River stared at her, confused and hurt. He opened his mouth to protest, but Ellie worked fast.

"I'm sorry," she whispered, brushing her hands from the crown of his head to his throat. His eyes closed, and his body stilled in her arms. Ellie struggled to untangle herself from the statue he'd become.

He stood there; his eyes closed as the spell passed through his body. He would wake again in a few moments, and it pained her to think of it. Her heart begged her to stay, but she didn't. She wouldn't allow herself to ruin another life with her mistake.

Chapter Fifteen

River lifted his head from his desk. His eyes blinked rapidly as he massaged his sore neck. He felt strange. Why had he fallen asleep? He'd slept well the night before; it made no sense why he needed an afternoon nap. He wore the black cardigan he kept in his office, but he didn't remember putting it on. He looked for his shirt and found it in the trash. His shirt had a ripped sleeve and was covered in dirt and blood.

He tried to remember his dream. It felt so real, more real than any dream he'd had before. He remembered Ellie, but the harder he tried to remember, the faster the dream seemed to slip away. Soon he would forget about Ellie altogether.

He got up, stretching his arms, and winced as a sharp pain pulsed in his left forearm. He walked out of his office and into the bathroom. Taking off the cardigan, he was surprised to see his upper arm bandaged up. What had happened? What was the last thing he remembered? He'd gone out to lunch, and then... a blank. There was nothing there. A dark hole where a memory should have been. He was still hungry, so he was sure he hadn't gotten his lunch. He checked his watch; six in the evening. He had lost more time.

The bandage covered his entire forearm. While he needed to keep the dressing on, he wanted to check what had happened to him. He unwrapped the gauze gingerly, sucking in air as it pulled against the wound. His confusion only grew when he saw three large lacerations on his arm. The middle gash was the longest by at least two inches, with the outside wounds being shorter and less deep. It didn't look like a knife wound. Skin carved by a knife was usually straight, clean, especially if they were sharp. They normally weren't this deep.

Once, in the early days of his career as a medical examiner, the police had brought in the body of a hiker. Found before the animals ate the rest of his body, River made out the unmistakable evidence of claw marks. He deduced the claws belonged to a mountain lion. Their force and speed created even jagged, deep wounds all over the hiker's body. His gashes looked similar to the hiker's, only the claw marks on him were longer, and he only counted three.

River took the time to clean out his wound again and dressed it. He found the task tedious and difficult, but he wasn't sure that he or someone else had done it well enough the first time around. He was losing time and his mind now, but he knew someone had to have helped him. The dressing before was too neat to be of his own doing.

River went back to his office and examined the remains of his shirt, tattered and covered in what he presumed to be his blood.

Every story that he could think of ran through his head. Trying to create a plausible scenario where any of this made sense. Each story was more bizarre than the first. He sat back in the chair, taking a deep breath to steady himself. He smelled something odd. A woody vanilla, he knew that scent…

A knock on his door interrupted his thoughts.

"Come in," he croaked out, clearing his throat. Brian walked in, pulling his scrubs over his clothes. If he found it strange that River was shirtless except for the cardigan, he didn't say it.

"You're still here?" Brian asked.

"Yes, but I'm on my way out."

"Well, you might have to stay a little longer. The police just brought in a body. They found it by the woods."

"Can't it wait until tomorrow?"

"I don't think so. The police think there is a serial killer out there killing women. They just want us to check if this is the same cause of death as the others. We can do the full report tomorrow." Brian left, and River walked over to the file cabinet where he kept an extra pair of scrubs and suited up.

He joined Brian in the examination room. The police were gone, and he stood on the other side of the body. Brian noted down the time on the examination sheet, and River unzipped the bag. As he pulled the zipper exposing the woman's naked body, he had to steady himself by what he saw. The same three long gashes on his arm were present throughout her body. A long middle slice, surrounded by two shorter lacerations on either side. A cluster around her neck would have been the primary cause of her death, but he noticed some on her chest, her arms, legs, and her abdomen. Her intestines poured out of her stomach, the mesentery membrane sliced through. He'd been lucky, he realized; it had sliced him the one time. This woman, however, wasn't as lucky.

"Looks like the cops were premature on this one. An animal of some sort, wouldn't you guess?" asked Brian, examining the markings.

"Yes."

"It's in clusters of three, and the skin pulled as the claws dragged." Brian's voice was even unaffected by yet another death, but River couldn't bring himself to say a word. Brian pulled her arm towards the light. "It looks like the animal has very curved claws. What kind of animal has only three claws?"

"A bird," said River.

"Well, unless there are ostriches around, I can't imagine there's a bird on the east coast with talons this big," said Brian.

River didn't respond, but he knew the lacerations could only have been done by bird talons. His hand touched his own injured arm.

What had he done in the last few hours?

CHAPTER SIXTEEN

Something was wrong with her. Kissing River in the same morgue she'd stolen Derek's body from a few weeks ago? What if they got caught? Or someone recognized her from the camera footage? She had cast a few occlusion spells, but she was stressed that night; it wouldn't surprise her if she'd missed something.

Stupid.

Stupid, but thrilling.

Even as she lay in bed two days later, waiting for Derek to join her, she still couldn't stop thinking about it. The feel of him. The way her thoughts quieted down the moment he held her. The concern in his eyes as she explained everything. He wasn't scared of her. He didn't back away and start lobbing accusations or calling the cops. The only thing he seemed to care about was her.

In the days that followed, Ellie couldn't let herself indulge in thoughts about him. She'd made the right choice in erasing his memories, and hopefully he would move on. But his warning rang in her head. How much could he know? She had a lot to do to add a concerned but also kind of handsome medical examiner into her life.

Violet hadn't returned to work for the past two days, giving Ellie plenty of time to convince herself that her story was a lie. But trying to decipher which parts were lies was the tough part.

Okay, so she knew about Paradise, but Ellie didn't for a second believe her about why she'd killed him. Not to mention, if what she said was true, Ellie had been working with a murderer for weeks. Violet never gave off the vibe that she was anything but a typical law student.

Also, Derek was acting normal again. He'd come home from work in a cheery mood. He would tell her about his day and crack an inside joke, making her laugh. It was just like in the past. Why believe some absurd story from Violet, when the proof she needed was right in front of her?

The creatures were a whole other matter. The only comfort she had was that she hadn't seen them since that day at her internship. She looked everywhere for them, unable to stop herself whenever she left the house. But she no longer saw their inky black feathers or their haunting blank stares. It didn't completely soothe her frayed nerves, but it was enough to survive.

Derek came out of the bathroom and settled in next to her, pulling her in tight. Ellie shivered without meaning to. His skin was still so cold.

"Are you sleepy?" she asked. For the past two days, he had slept with her the entire night. She kept waking up every few hours and turning to him, only to fall back into fitful sleep when she saw him there.

"Not really, but I'm trying."

"Maybe you'll sleep tonight?"

"I'm not sure I will. What if I never go back to normal?"

Ellie's heart skipped a beat. No, she needed normalcy more than anything else. Even if it hadn't been perfect. "It's taking a while for your body to adjust."

"It's been weeks now. I'm not hungry or thirsty. I'm never tired."

"Are you feeling okay though?"

"What do you mean?"

She remembered his hands around her neck. "Emotionally? Are you sadder or more frustrated?" Or angrier, but she didn't want to suggest that.

Derek hesitated. "I'm more... me."

She couldn't understand what he meant. "Is that a bad thing?"

"Depends on the person, I guess."

"Is it bad for you?"

He stared at her with an intensity that made her skin crawl. "No."

With a quick peck on her lips, he turned and shut off the lamp. But Ellie didn't sleep. She closed her eyes and stayed stock-still, breathing heavily like she would when she slept. She needed to pretend. Unsure of why, but the sensation wouldn't leave her. The night already seemed weird to her. Something told her she shouldn't doze off tonight.

She wasn't sure how much time had passed, or how long she'd been pretending, but the bed dipped as Derek got up. She didn't open her eyes, but heard the closet light turn on, accompanied by the sound of a zipper being pulled. Then after a moment, the soft click of the lock from the front door.

She shot up but didn't linger in the room. She quickly changed into a tracksuit she'd stashed under the bed, threw on some sneakers and followed him out.

Violet was wrong. She was going to prove it.

Chapter Seventeen

As River handed his credit card to the bartender, he tried his best to make do with the crappy situation his gift had pulled him into. The bartender slid a beer into his hand, and River turned back to the throng of people dancing. A few of the girls on the floor eyed him, no doubt trying to find the courage to approach him. It was sheer luck that he'd worn something other than scrubs that day, because he was sure the bouncer wouldn't have let him in looking like he'd just finished a shift at the hospital.

He didn't want to be there. Nothing seemed worse than spending an evening at a sweaty and loud club. But he had no choice. As soon as he stepped into his car, he felt a twinge in his chest telling him to get out and walk down the few blocks that led him straight to the club. He could go home now. His gift had stopped when he walked through the door. But he stayed, getting the sense that what he needed to see still hadn't arrived.

For the past few nights, everything had gone back to normal. He hadn't lost more time, which he was thankful for, but something still felt off. But the more he tried to figure it out, the further the answer got away from him.

If his gift wanted him at a club, then who was he to fight it? Nothing was out of the ordinary. It was like any other club. The same kind of people, the same music, the same overpriced beer.

But then he turned and saw her.

Ellie, with her brown hair tied in a ponytail, arms wrapped around herself as if she was cold. She scanned every face in the place until she recognized him. She tried to run off, but he was much faster. He grabbed her arm and was surprised when she didn't pull away.

"Hey," he said. Not quite the way he would have wanted to start the reunion, but then again it had been at least a week since he'd seen her last at school.

"Please, River. Not now."

The music was getting too loud, so he motioned with his head towards the outdoor balcony, but Ellie stayed firmly planted. "I need to apologize," he said, leaning down to her ear. "I didn't mean to scare you."

"I know," she said. "Trust me."

"I have these drea—"

"Dreams! I know okay! My boyfriend was dead! Now he's not! I'm in danger, and all you want to do is be nice and save me! I get it!"

River was dumbfounded, and the only thing he could muster was a faint, "Okay."

"Can you let me go now? I'm kind of in the middle of something."

He did, but he didn't leave her side. As she snaked her way through the crowd, she didn't reprimand him for being her shadow. Once she finished her round through the club and headed to the bathrooms, she finally turned to him.

"Can you check the men's bathroom?"

"For who?"

"You know who."

Right. Dead man. He did as she asked, but found no one there. As he reported it, she responded with a heavy sigh.

"I lost him."

"Why were you tailing him?"

"He's my boyfriend."

That stung. He wasn't sure why, but it did. He saw them kiss. What did he expect just because he was dreaming about her, the real Ellie would want him? "Do you want to get some fresh air?"

She stared at him for a moment, contemplating her choices, but she nodded, loosening the tense knot in his chest he hadn't even noticed was there.

Outside on the balcony and away from the crowd, he breathed easier. A quick glance at her though, and he realized he was the only one who felt better.

"Do you want to explain why your boyfriend came back from the dead a few weeks ago, and now you're chasing him through clubs?"

"River, if I did, nothing would change between us."

He had no clue what she meant by that. Her entire demeanor was so off to what he'd experienced at school and in his dreams. What if he was mistaken about her? "So, you knew your boyfriend was dead."

"Yes."

"So my warning—"

"It was nice of you, but unnecessary. I can handle it."

"What do you mean, handle it? Is something wrong?"

Ellie bit her lip, and for the first time all night, the version of her he saw in his dreams came out. All the tense worry drained out, replaced by the vulnerable stare he was used to in his dreams.

"Nothing's wrong."

"Why are you lying?"

"God, you always do that."

"Now I'm really confused."

"You think you know me."

"I get it. I don't. But I can tell that something's wrong. Even now, as you keep lying."

"I'm not lying to you."

River grew frustrated. "You're nothing like I thought you were going to be."

"Have you been following me?"

"In a manner of speaking."

"What?"

"I've had dreams about you."

Instead of appearing alarmed, she looked curious. "What kind of dreams?"

"Just you. Sometimes we're at school. Other times we're in my apartment."

"What are we doing?"

As if he were about to detail his wet dreams to her. "Talking."

"About what?"

"You really want the details, don't you?"

"You can't drop 'I have dreams about you,' and then expect me not to be curious."

"Good point." River looked over the balcony, finding her intense gaze uncomfortable. "For the longest time, you would ask questions about me. It was like you wanted to learn everything about me or something. Other times, I try to get information from you, but you're as evasive in my dreams as you are in person. Sometimes we would talk about your... boyfriend." He said the term as if it burned his tongue.

"You keep surprising me," she said after a moment.

"I don't understand?"

"I'm trying so hard right now, to not fuck up your life."

"What?"

"I don't want you in my mess."

"What if I want to be there?"

"Then you are as stupid as you are selfless."

"Ouch."

"Sorry."

"Truth is, I kind of don't care." He wasn't sure when he'd gotten closer. He didn't even realize she'd closed the distance further.

"River," she said his name slowly, a warning to stop them both. "Think about this for one second. You know nothing about me except that my boyfriend was dead. I'm in deep trouble, but I can't tell you any of it. Not without putting you in danger."

"Are you trying to scare me off?"

"Yes. And I have no clue why it's not working."

"Me neither."

If she hadn't kissed him, he would have done it. Her lips were on his before he could take a breath in shock. She was solid in his arms, nothing like his dreams. She was so much softer, and her grip stronger, surprising him with how tightly she held on to him. His surroundings dissolved, and he focused only on her. The universe could've disappeared, and he wouldn't have even noticed.

Chapter Eighteen

E llie was the first to initiate the kiss, and even though she didn't want to, she was the first to pull away. His stare was a mix of awe and hunger. He glanced at her lips, about to dive right back in when she stepped away.

No, this wasn't good. She shouldn't have kissed him the first time at the morgue. She could excuse that moment after the adrenaline rush of running from the creatures and Violet's revelation.

This kiss? She had no excuse that would explain it. She just wanted to. As soon as she saw him at the club, all she wanted was to wrap her arms around him and see if the previous kiss and touch still felt the same. And it did. The peace and stillness were such a welcome break that to pull away from it now felt like skydiving out of a plane.

"What was that?" he asked.

Right. He didn't have his memories. The jury was still out if she would let him keep these. "Nothing."

"That didn't mean nothing."

"I have to get out of here."

"Wait, tell me what's going on at least. I can help you."

"You don't get it. And you can't get it. Ever. Not because you wouldn't understand. Something tells me you would, but I can't hurt you."

"Why would you hurt me?"

She reached out and touched the arm that she had mended just a few days ago. Remembering the blood of that day, and trying her best to clean the wound made her nauseas even now. "I've already hurt you."

"How do you know about that?" he asked.

"Don't worry about it. But it's the reason I can't tell you more. I'm sorry."

She turned away from him and froze. Derek stood in the doorway. His expression was unreadable, but that made it all the more terrifying.

She tried to approach him, but in a flash he ran out ahead of her. She took off after him, dodging and weaving through the crowd, but by the time she got outside the club he was gone. She searched left and right, but there was no sign of him in either direction.

"Hey," River grabbed her hand, and the contact made her jump. "Are you okay?"

"You saw him, didn't you?"

"Of course."

"I have to go. He's not going to be happy."

"Wait, are you sure it's safe? What if he does something?"

"Like what?" She tried to play it off like it was ridiculous for him to suggest such a thing, but her mind flashed to the night Derek's hands wrapped around her throat. She shivered, but it wasn't because she was cold.

"Look, I don't know him like that, but I'm worried about you."

"I'll be fine."

"You're lying. What has he done to you?"

Ellie panicked. "Nothing."

"No, you're not safe if you go back. Come with me. At least for tonight."

It was so tempting. She had no clue what awaited her at home. She didn't even know whether Derek would return to their apartment at all. But the situation didn't change because of one kiss. Well, a second kiss.

She pulled River along the street, and into the first alleyway she found. Although he seemed confused, he didn't say a word or fight her. She peered down the way, making sure no one was near, and the drunken crowd around them were too preoccupied with getting home to pay them much attention.

"Ellie, what is it?"

She didn't answer in words. She couldn't anymore. No matter how many times she explained, he was too stubborn to get it. She stood on her toes and kissed him again. Thankfully, he was too happy to play along with her plan.

As soon as lips touched hers, every fear and worry washed away from her. Her problems floated further from her, and she wanted nothing more than to continue kissing him if it meant she didn't have to deal with them. But it wasn't fair to River.

His hands cupped her face, and the tenderness he had with her made her want to cry out. He was too wrapped up in her and completely unaware that she wouldn't let him keep this memory either.

Chapter Nineteen

E llie settled deeper into her bathtub. The water rose to her chin. Her eyes ached from crying, and she hoped a cleansing bath would help.

Ellie arrived back home from the club and found herself in an empty apartment. She waited for Derek to come home and dreaded the conversation they would have. How could she explain what he'd seen at the club? But then again, what was he doing there?

But she fell asleep before she could have that conversation. When she woke up, he still wasn't home. A couple of ignored phone calls later, and she realized he wouldn't be coming home.

She felt dirty, like something clung to her. A sticky energy of sorts. She had filled the tub with scalding hot water and poured hyssop and rosemary into the bath. She hoped to calm herself down from her night and for the water to carry away the energy.

The tea-like scent of the herbs in her bath made her relax a little, but it wasn't working as well as she wanted. River floated into her mind no matter how hard she tried to push him away. She thought of how he looked slumped over on his desk as she sneaked out of the morgue. How he stood, eyes closed, leaning against the alley wall, giving her enough time to leave. Of the conversations at school and the way his lips felt against hers. Her skin flowered into goosebumps at the thought of his hands on her. What was wrong with her?

She got out of the bath and let the herbs flow down the drain as she got dressed. She hoped the bath would be all that she needed, but something was still wrong. Like she was walking during an earthquake, her steps unsteady on the loosening ground.

Ellie walked into the kitchen and opened the fridge. Searching its contents, she found what she was looking for: a carton of eggs. She pulled out only one, letting it sit on a towel on the counter as she filled a clear glass with water. She ran the egg across her body, starting from the top of her head, sweeping the energy downwards to the soles of her feet. She closed her eyes while she did it, asking whatever clung to be released from her. When she finished, she cracked the egg into the glass of water.

She set the glass on the counter and got on her knees to read the cleanse. Sometimes, as her mother had once explained, the floating whites would form into the face of the person who tormented you. She couldn't see a face, but there were three streaks of red on the yolk — blood. Small bubbles started to form and float towards the surface. But the bubbles stopped floating midway through the glass. The cleansing ritual hadn't been enough. The blood in the yolk was an ominous sign.

Ellie shook as she threw the egg down the drain with the water. She ran to her room and grabbed the box in her closet again. She may not be the best tarot reader, but she needed something, anything, to help her understand what was happening.

While she shuffled, two cards flew out. The King of Pentacles and the Emperor reversed. She understood now — River the King, and Derek the Emperor.

She kept shuffling, whispering to herself, "The next card will represent me. What shall I do?" She stopped shuffling and pulled the first card on the top, the Devil. She tried to remember what it meant.

Her mother used to read the cards fluently. Their meanings were etched in her brain. It wasn't the first time Ellie had gotten the Devil. During her mother's readings, it popped up on more than one occasion. What had her mother told her about it? She couldn't remember. What she remembered was the smell of chiles, freshly charred, over the stove. The sound of the Latine news playing in the background floated into her mind. Her mother's brow furrowed as she pored over Ellie's cards. Ellie stared at the faint lines around her mouth. A permanent imprint of her smile. Her anxiety grew the longer her mother stared at her cards.

"See this," she pointed at the Devil. "You are holding yourself back."

"The Diablo is holding me back, Mom." Ellie pointed to the chains around the necks of the two figures below the devil.

The devil's horned visage, with its pointed tongue hanging out, freaked her out.

"No, it's you. You can get out of these chains. You can set yourself free. This here," she said, pointing to the devil. Her nails clicked on the card. "This is your fear. This is not outside yourself; it's you."

Violet's words earlier that morning were ringing in her ears. *'How well do you know him?'* She had lied when she told Violet that she knew him well. She should know him well by now. But there were always holes in his stories. Large vacuous holes that Ellie tried her best not to peer into. Derek not telling her about what he was doing at Paradise the night of his death wasn't anything new. Late nights where she grasped cold sheets next to her weren't new.

Ellie didn't want to cause problems. She wanted him to be *it*. She wanted him to be everything that she would need, even if there were problems she had to overlook. She had no one, and if he left, what was she to do? So, she ignored the problems, the lies, and she would sacrifice herself and her happiness if it meant she wouldn't sleep alone. Why could he never do the same?

Enter River Mathews. River with the soft eyes and tender touch. The man who would help her when he had no reason to. She didn't even know him, and yet he felt... right.

Guilt squirmed in her for erasing his memory twice, but the creature attack solidified her plan. She wouldn't drag him into this world. She wouldn't put him in danger again. Maybe he was the person for her in the end? Just her luck. If she hadn't brought back her ex, she would've been single. She choked out a laugh at that.

She called Derek but wasn't surprised when he didn't answer. There was a change in him. She massaged her neck, remembering the fear when he had choked her as a joke. Her instincts had been screaming at her since she'd brought him back. She realized now that the same instincts had been yelling at her for the two years they'd been together. It was only now that she could no longer ignore them.

Her instincts now led her to the only thing she didn't want to do. She didn't have a choice anymore.

She scrolled through her phone and found Violet's number. Violet answered on the first ring, as if she had been waiting by her phone for days for this call.

"Hello? Ellie?"

"Hi…"

"Are you okay?"

"I'm fine," she lied. Her hands shook. Why was this so difficult? "I need your help."

CHAPTER TWENTY

Ellie parked her car outside of Books & Beans. She looked out the window for any signs of River. There were a few people still around, congregated in the gazebo and sitting on the park benches. The morgue closed at five. River would be home by now. At least she hoped.

She had never been inside Books & Beans before, but the warm and cozy ambiance of the place charmed her. It smelled divine, like coffee and cinnamon rolls. The wooden shelves were filled to the brim with books. She would have loved to explore a place like this before, but she didn't have time to peek around now. Violet approached her first, rising from a stool by the counter.

"Ellie, this is Margaret," she said as a woman with long red hair and freckles all over her body shook her hand. "And this is Molly." She pointed to a black woman with a halo of brown curly hair, who stood behind the counter. Ellie thought Molly looked uneasy. She dried mugs with a dish towel and nodded in their direction. Ellie gave a half-hearted wave and said hello, unsure of what else to say.

"Lock the door, Violet," said Molly. Ellie's heart dipped as Violet walked past her to the door. "What's going on, girls?" asked Molly as soon as the lock clicked shut. Ellie noticed Margaret looking down at the floor and wondered if she should say something.

"Before you get upset, just know I had the best intentions," Violet began.

"I already hate where this is going," as Molly stopped drying the mugs, Ellie noticed her brows raised higher towards her hairline.

"Margaret and I... killed a man." If Molly looked worried before, it was nothing compared to how she looked now.

"We killed a man and, turns out, it was Ellie's boyfriend," Violet continued, motioning to Ellie. While Margaret looked like she was about to cry, Violet didn't appear apologetic at all. She didn't turn away from Molly.

"Why?" was all that Molly could ask in her shock.

"He almost killed Maggie!"

"Is this true?" Molly asked Margaret.

"Of course, it's true!" Violet answered.

"I'm asking Margaret!"

"I was at Paradise," Margaret began, and Ellie's head snapped to her. "He was flirting with me and buying me drinks. And he was so interested in talking to me, I... I don't know. Maybe I was just too excited or stupid. Maybe I didn't pay attention..." her voice warbled.

"He asked if I wanted to go back to his place, and I thought, why not, you know? Just something stupid and fun. So, he drove us to the woods near the hiking trail. I was kind of confused, but I thought he had a cabin or something. And we started walking deep into the forest, and I started getting scared. I wanted to go back, but he kept saying, a little farther. He was so insistent, but I knew something was wrong, and I told him I was going back. That's when it started..." Margaret started crying then, and Violet placed her hand on her shoulder, keeping her close.

"How did you know where Margaret was?" asked Molly.

"I was at home studying when I felt like something was wrong," said Violet. "And then I had a vision, I think. I'm not really sure. It's the first premonition I've ever had. But I saw Maggie in the forest with this man. I saw they were near Oakway Bridge, and so I just got into my car and drove like hell. I ran into her on the bridge, like in my vision. The guy was right behind her, and I didn't have time to think. I just hit him."

"With what?" asked Molly.

"A rock."

"Is that how he died? A rock to the head?" asked Molly.

Violet hesitated, and Ellie noticed Margaret shook as she cried harder. "We knew the coven would never approve..."

"Violet?"

"Lola's family spell book has death spells. We got it out of there, and we cast the spell later that night." Violet stood defiantly, waiting for Molly to chastise her. Molly looked closer to a nervous breakdown than to lashing out. "Lola doesn't know we used the spell," Violet quickly added.

"Violet, this coven has rules for a reason! To keep us safe! To keep us hidden! You could have exposed us or worse!" Ellie could now understand why Margaret didn't look her in the eyes. Some mugs on the wall around Molly shook. Ellie didn't blame her for being angry. She got the sense that Molly was probably often tasked with cleaning up everyone's mess. Now Ellie had brought in another problem.

"Well, it's worse now," Violet said.

"Meaning?"

"Meaning, Ellie resurrected her boyfriend."

"Are you kidding?" Molly turned towards Ellie, and she wanted to shrink back and hide. "You resurrected him?"

"Yes."

"With what spell?"

"A spell from my family's book."

"What was involved?"

"What?"

"What was in the spell?"

"Uh... white candles, frankincense oil, some water that had a rose of Jericho in it, mixed with yew and blood."

"Whose blood?"

"Mine."

"Goddess, you're a fool."

"Hey," interrupted Violet. "Come on, Molly, she needs our help!"

"There's nothing we can do."

"There has to be something!"

"Death cannot be cheated, and it named a price." Molly looked at Ellie; the pity in her eyes stung. "She bound his soul to hers. If we kill him, she will die."

"That can't be true. There has to be another way," said Violet.

"We can ask the others," Margaret piped up. "Somebody must know something!"

"This coven is a democracy," Violet said. "We're supposed to vote on huge spells and decisions like this."

"Which you two didn't consider when you killed her boyfriend," Molly reminded them.

"Still, let's ask the others. If they all vote not to help, then fine, but let's vote on it." Violet argued.

Ellie could tell that beneath Molly's anger lay fear. Ellie didn't blame her for that. For years now, they had been dragging witches to court. Neighborhood mobs attacked the unlucky ones, ready to rip them limb from limb with no evidence at all. 'Thou shall not suffer a witch to live.' And they lived by it. Ellie knew that by helping her, Molly and the rest of the coven were a step closer to exposure, and a step closer to death.

"We need to take care of a few things first," Molly began. "Where is your book?" she asked Ellie.

"At home."

"Bring it. Where is your boyfriend?"

"I don't know. He hasn't been himself lately."

"Meaning?"

"I didn't know about his secret life," Ellie turned to Margaret, meeting two large, teary eyes. To think that he was going to hurt her, or that he could hurt anyone, scared her. "He's been acting more erratic, angrier. I don't know if I did the working right because his energy has been off these past few weeks."

"When you brought back his soul, he had already gone to the other side. Who knows how many souls he tormented he met over there?" Molly said.

"Wouldn't that mean he would be nicer? I mean, to meet the people you've killed, shouldn't you be remorseful or something?" asked Violet.

"I guess he wasn't remorseful," said Molly.

"Wait, you guys think he's done this before?" asked Ellie.

"Come on, Ellie," said Violet, "how many murdered women have they been finding lately?"

"Forget lately, what about the past three years?" said Molly. "They've found at least one murdered woman every couple of months. It's ramped up as of late, but yes, I think he's done this before."

Ellie's mind flashed to the other night when his hands gripped around her throat. How many times had he done that? His grip had been so sure, so steady. Knowing where to put the pressure to close her windpipe faster as she struggled. Ellie's heart started hammering. The blood rushed to her head, making her ears ring. She felt woozy, off balance, and she looked to the couches wondering which one she could get to the fastest.

"Ellie?" Violet asked, but she sounded so far away.

"Grab her," said Molly.

Ellie was aware of two pairs of hands holding her arms, and she sat on the brown leather couch closest to her. Her breathing got stuck between her lungs and her mouth, and her hands shook in her lap.

"How could I not have known?" She said mostly to herself. But saw in her periphery Molly and Violet looking at each other, unsure of how to answer. "Was I that stupid?"

"You're not stupid, Ellie," said Violet, crouching down next to her. "You're not stupid. Okay. He's good at fooling people. Look at Maggie. He fooled her. He knows how to manipulate people to get what he wants. But it has nothing to do with you."

Ellie looked at Violet, her face blurry beneath her tears. How could she be so kind to her? After Ellie ignored her at their internship and classes. After everything she'd done. Unleashing Derek back into the world. Causing more destruction and killing countless more women. Goddess, she was selfish. She should have let Derek stay dead.

Ellie's breath steadied after a moment. The warmth of the coffee shop and the steady sound of a clock ticking nearby grounded her. She didn't want to fall apart now. She had made this mess. She needed to be strong and set things right. Molly, Margaret, and Violet's presence comforted her. Yet again, strangers came to her aid. She wouldn't let them be strangers anymore.

"What do I do?" she asked.

Molly hesitated for a moment, but with a heavy sigh said, "We need something personal of his if you can't find him. Hair would be ideal. We need everything you used for the spell and your mom's book. Violet, go with Ellie to grab what she needs. Margaret and I will meet you back at the house."

"You'll help me?" asked Ellie.

"Yes," said Molly. She didn't elaborate further.

"There's one more thing," interrupted Ellie. Molly gave her a look that groaned, 'What now?' "I'm being followed by some creatures. I've never seen them before. They look like giant vultures. They have black feathered coats and long talons. Have you ever heard of such a creature?"

"Not off the top of my head, but it's important then that you get to my house as fast as you can."

Ellie wanted to thank her. Thank all of them, but they started moving. Violet motioned for her to come to the door, and Molly and Margaret were already walking to the back of the coffee shop. She had no clue how she would ever repay them.

Chapter Twenty-One

They arrived at her apartment a few minutes later. Violet pulled into the spot next to her and got out of her car. Ellie led the way. With any luck, Derek wouldn't be home. Ellie checked her phone for the time, trying to guess if she would bump into him. It wasn't late, but it didn't matter anymore since he no longer kept to his usual schedule.

As they walked towards her apartment, Ellie stopped abruptly, bringing Violet to a halt next to her. Her door stood slightly ajar, its welcome mat darkened by blood. Large black feathers were stuck on the mat, as well as on the concrete leading to her apartment.

"Is that..." Violet began.

"I'm not sure."

"It looks like the feathers of the creature from this morning," said Violet.

They had no other choice but to walk into the apartment. They needed the book. Violet pushed the front door ajar, and Ellie reached in to switch on the light. Ellie half-expected something to jump out, but her living room was empty. They walked through the door, but Violet left it open, just in case they needed to make a quick getaway.

"Derek?" called out Ellie, to no answer.

She sidestepped the living room carpet, marred with dark red stains. The smell of iron and salt was thick in the air.

"I don't think anyone is here," said Violet. "Let's just get what we need and leave."

"But there's blood, Violet. What if the creature hurt Derek?"

"I don't want to stay here long enough to find out."

Ellie nodded, and she rushed into her bedroom. She noticed the bloodstains on her carpet were bigger and wetter near the kitchen, but she had no time to investigate it. She checked the adjoining bathroom, finding it empty. Relief swept through her realizing they were alone, and she got to work. She reached into her closet and pulled out the box that contained the last of her magical items. She took the entire box, not wanting to leave it all behind. The bathroom was next, and she grabbed Derek's comb. His blond strands knotted within the comb's teeth. She went into the kitchen, putting the box on the one spot on the floor that didn't have blood on it.

"You got everything?" asked Violet.

"Almost." Ellie opened the drawers in her kitchen, trying to find a plastic bag to put Derek's comb in, when she heard Violet gasp.

Ellie looked up and froze at the familiar silhouette of Derek in the doorway. He trudged into the apartment. His eyes were red, strained out of their eye sockets. His breathing came out slow and shallow. Foam fell from his mouth in thick suds.

"Derek?" called out Ellie after a moment.

"Stop it!" snapped Violet. "Look at him! That's not Derek."

Derek sauntered further into the room, and it was only then that Ellie saw the claws. Three long claws sprouted from where his fingers should have been. They curved inward, their tips black. Derek didn't even notice Violet, as his eyes were fixed on Ellie alone. He walked even closer, but stopped in the middle of the living room. Ellie's heart raced; they were cornered.

Violet moved behind Ellie and opened the closet, looking for another exit. Violet screamed behind her, and when Ellie whipped around, she saw a body fall out of the pantry. A woman with vacant eyes stared at the ceiling. She still wore her jogging outfit, her dark hair still in a tight ponytail. Her throat looked shredded; her head was barely attached to her neck by a small plinth of flesh.

It was then that Ellie heard Derek moving. She looked up, only to see him barreling towards them. Violet thought more quickly on her feet. She grabbed a knife from the open drawer and started slicing through the air.

Derek dodged the knife. He pounced, trying to grab it from Violet's hands, but she moved faster and sliced his arm. Derek stepped back, a howl coming from his mouth.

"Whatever he is, he's not human anymore!" yelled Violet over the howls.

He looked up again and placed his sights on Ellie. She looked for a weapon. Anything to stop him, but he ran and lunged himself at her. Instinctively, Ellie raised her hands to cover herself. She walked back, tripped over her own feet, and fell hard on her back. She heard a crash, like glass breaking over hard tile.

The claws never came, nor did the pain. She tentatively pulled her arms away from her face and saw Derek slumped on the ground. River stood behind him with a broken lamp in his hands.

Chapter Twenty-Two

River could've never guessed where he was headed when he stepped into his car. Just like the night a few days before, when he awoke in the middle of the alley unsure why or how he got there. He knew he had gone to the club, but then nothing. Nothing at all. Perhaps it was this distraction; his insistence on trying to use logic to piece together his disjointed day that led him to an apartment complex he had never been to before.

He cursed under his breath, upset with himself that he hadn't been paying attention while driving. He could have gotten into a wreck, or hurt someone, but he cut his self-flagellation short when he saw the dead man walking across the parking lot.

His feet dragged across the pavement as he lumbered forward. In the low light of a lonely street lamp, River couldn't make him out too well, but the guy wasn't well. He needed to follow him. His gift brought him here, but he wanted to turn his car back on and leave like a coward. He watched as the man reached the apartment complex. He muttered a 'fuck it' under his breath and unbuckled his seat belt.

River waited until he had cleared the parking lot to step out of his car. He didn't want to follow too closely, and the man moved at a slow pace. He followed a few paces behind and tried to remain as quiet as possible. He waited until the man had cleared the stairs before he climbed them. It turned out to be a terrible mistake. He lost him on the second floor.

Swearing to himself, River closed his eyes, trying to will his gift to work. He had never used it this way, and if he was honest with himself, he had never wanted to. He'd been too afraid of what his gift would show him. More things that he couldn't change or knowledge he didn't want to know. But he squeezed his eyes shut. Nothing came to him. His gift wasn't radar, but he pleaded with his mind to give anything, but all he found was dread and an anxiety that choked his heart.

His eyes snapped open at a sudden piercing scream echoing down the hallway. River had no time to think. He reacted, tearing down the hallway. He saw an open door. There was no time to examine the bloody footprints or feathers strewn about the entrance. The dead man lifted his arms, and River reached for the only thing near him, a heavy porcelain lamp, and struck him on the head.

When the man fell, River was surprised to see Ellie on the floor. She looked frightened, her chest heaving up and down, tears welling up in her eyes. Where was he? He reached out his hand to help her up. She stared at his outstretched hand for a moment before hesitantly accepting his help.

"What are you doing here?" she asked.

River wanted to explain that he had no clue. He didn't even know where he was. But he wasn't sure how to describe what he was.

"I followed you," he lied.

"You have a stalker on top of everything else?" River turned to Violet, unaware that there was anyone else there besides Ellie and the unconscious man at his feet. Something else caught his eye that shook his body to the core. Lying motionless on the floor was another woman, her body and clothes soaked in blood.

"Oh, my God." He kneeled by the woman's body, feeling her wrist for a pulse even though from the dried injuries he could tell she had been dead for a few hours. He took a preliminary examination of her corpse, noticing large wide lesions reminiscent of the body he had examined in the morgue earlier. The same injuries that he'd found on his own arm.

"We need to call the police." He started taking out his phone when Violet snatched it from his hands.

"You can't do that," she said.

"Violet, wait..." Ellie started.

"He can't! What would we tell them?"

"We tell them what happened," said River.

"This is my apartment," explained Ellie. "We came here to grab some things, but when we arrived, we saw someone had trashed the place. Blood was everywhere, and Violet opened the closet and this woman..." Ellie choked on her last words.

River got up from where he kneeled. He yearned to reach out and embrace her, to stop her tears and comfort her, but he held himself back. This wasn't the time. There was a corpse and an unconscious man that he had just assaulted that they needed to deal with first.

"That's when Derek came home and, well, you know the rest."

"I don't understand. Why can't we call the cops? Or even an ambulance for him," he said, pointing to Derek's slumped form on the floor. "He probably has a concussion."

"We can't River. Look at how this looks. They'll take me in for questioning, and I don't have any answers for them. I couldn't explain this even if I tried, and if I told the truth..." she stopped herself.

"Tell the truth about what?" River noticed Violet had gotten closer to Ellie.

"I think Derek killed this woman," said Ellie.

"That's not possible," said River. "Look at her lesions. See how they're jagged? An animal did this."

"An animal that stuffed her in the closet?" asked Ellie. River had no answer for that.

"We don't have time for this," said Violet. "Look, we'll figure out what to do with her body later. We can't leave her here, but we can't take her with us either. But we should take him," she pointed at Derek. Violet spoke as if River wasn't in the room.

"We can't move the body; that's evidence. If someone planted her, the police will figure out who did it, and they won't pin it on you."

"Please," scoffed Violet. "You have no clue about what we're dealing with here. Don't you get it? The police are useless. They'll just complicate everything and throw us in jail. We're running out of time!" She said the last thing to Ellie, ignoring River again.

Ellie pressed her hands to her head, massaging her temples. River wanted her to explain. Nothing made sense. Until now, he had thought of her as an unsuspecting damsel, someone surrounded by danger that his gift pushed him to save, like all the others before her. Yet here she was, arguing with him to hide a murder. What had his gift gotten him into?

"River," she said. "I'm a witch."

What should have come as a shock, what should have floored him, didn't. All the jumbled pieces he had been trying to piece together in this scenario finally clicked into place.

"Of course," he said.

"I brought Derek back from the dead."

"You..."

"Violet and her friend killed him, and I brought him back. I stole him from the morgue, and took him to my apartment, and I resurrected him. But he hasn't been himself since the spell. He's meaner and crueler, and he's changing physically. He murdered this woman, and I'm pretty sure he's murdered more."

River didn't know what to say.

"Are you going to turn me in?" her voice faltered.

It hurt River that she would even suggest it. He knew the risks. The life of hiding who he really was. Ellie was no different. This was a mess, but during it, River had never felt happier.

"I would never turn you in." He reached out to hold her hands. They were cold against his palms. She didn't pull away, and it filled him with a warmth he didn't understand. "I don't think I can convince you in the next five minutes, but believe me."

Her brown eyes burrowed into his. She hesitated before whispering, "Okay."

He wanted to stay there with her. The others faded into the background when Ellie stood near him. Her hands fit perfectly in his, and he wanted to steady the tremor in them. Violet cleared her throat.

"Well, I don't trust you," said Violet. "And frankly, my dude, I wouldn't trust a guy who works with cops."

"I work at the morgue. I'm not a cop."

"Semantics. And not to ruin the mood, but we need to hurry," she said to Ellie.

Ellie hesitated, but she pulled her hands away from his. She left an emptiness in its place and an urge to hold her again.

They made a plan. They left the dead woman where she was. Violet explained they would get another coven member to move her later. They tied Derek up using duct tape. He hadn't woken up yet, but they wouldn't risk it. It was better to bring him along, afraid that if they left him behind, he would kill more people. River carried Derek's heavy body downstairs and into Violet's trunk.

Ellie worked with River to clean the blood from the doorway of her apartment. They had to not draw suspicion to the apartment. It was only a matter of time before this woman's family or friends started looking for her. How long until the police started connecting the dots to Derek? River knew they had little time to do what they had to. He needed to focus on the task at hand, but his eyes flickered to Ellie.

He had never been this close or been with her for this long. Ellie seemed to be more at ease with him. He didn't understand why, but he tried not to question it. He didn't want to question anything anymore. That was gone, and now that he had decided to listen to his gift first, he needed to flow with it. Not that it was easy, but this had worked out. Maybe everything else would, too.

"Why are you always around exactly when I need you?" she asked, breaking him away from his thoughts.

"It's hard to explain," but River reasoned, if anyone would understand, she would.

"Try."

Ellie looked at him with her big brown eyes. Her hair covered half her face, and she couldn't move it without smearing blood on her temple. He wanted to tuck it behind her ear, but he stopped himself.

River wanted to tell her everything. She had trusted him with her secret. He knew what she risked. She placed her life in his undeserving hands, to do with as he pleased. He could tell her everything, every thought, no matter how dark, and she would love him. The thought floated effortlessly into his mind.

Love? Is this what all this is about?

Before he could dissect it further, Violet walked in. "Everything's in the car. Let's go."

"I'll come with you," said River.

"No, you're not. Thank you for all your help," Violet reached out a hand as if to shake his, which he found odd and formal after all they'd been through. He reached out, but Ellie pulled his hand back.

"If I bring you along, will you tell me then?" asked Ellie. His whole body grew hot with her hand in his.

"Yes," he said.

CHAPTER TWENTY-THREE

Ellie sat on the passenger side of Violet's car. Her left arm itched, and she absentmindedly scratched it, watching the trees pass by her window. Her mind flitted to River, whose car she periodically checked in on using the side mirror. His headlights brought comfort, and she didn't understand why.

She had told him the truth. No use hiding it anymore. It was the third time she had felt compelled to tell him. That wasn't natural. She had kept the secret so close to her heart for so long. She had never been comfortable enough in her relationship with Derek to tell him, even after two years together. But then again, she hadn't told Derek much. Maybe she had always known that he couldn't be trusted. Yet, she wondered how she trusted a man she had only met a handful of times.

"How much do you know about this guy?" asked Violet, as if reading her mind. It was bizarre to Ellie how much she already trusted Violet, too. She had never been in a coven before. Her mother had always been a solo practitioner. Her family in Mexico practiced together, but few people outside of the family were aware of the witches among them. It was dangerous to have their business out there like that.

"I know his last name."

"That's it?"

"Well, he's the medical examiner. He was the one examining Derek's body in the morgue. He figured out that Derek was alive, and he found me to warn me about him." Violet didn't respond, a silence that urged Ellie to continue. "It sounds stupid, but when he's near, everything slows down. I can't describe it. Even with all this mess, I feel calm when I'm near him."

"So, you like him?"

"I don't know. I wouldn't say I 'like' him."

"Aren't you supposed to feel like butterflies in your stomach or something?"

"The exact opposite. All those things — butterflies, heart dropping into my stomach like I'm on a roller coaster — it doesn't feel like any of it. It just feels like..."

"Peace." Finished Violet for her.

"Is that weird?" Ellie's question was sincere. She had no frame of reference for this. In her previous relationships before Derek, she came to realize, had been much of the same. An endless lineup of men that made her nervous. Men who held onto her lightly while she clung on to them with all her strength. They dropped her like she was nothing, and thinking about the desperate attempts she made to keep them in her life made her cringe. Yet with River, she didn't have to hold on to him. She got the feeling that he would follow her anywhere she asked.

"Normally I wouldn't trust the whole love at first sight thing," said Violet. "But who knows? Maybe soulmates are real after all? You strike me as the romantic type."

"I'm not sure if I can trust the soulmate thing. My soulmate is tied up in the trunk."

"He is not your soulmate," said Violet, getting serious.

Ellie didn't answer. Ellie wanted to argue with her, tell her that for two years Derek was her soulmate. He was everything to her, and his coming back from the dead changed him. But she couldn't; doing so would make her unearth the red flags she buried long ago.

She wanted to change the subject. She didn't want to dwell on her past with Derek anymore.

"Who's in your coven? Is it just Molly and Margaret?"

"There's six of us, including me. Molly, Margaret, Rosie, Lenore, and Lola. Molly's the leader. Although it's not like we had a vote on it or anything. She's the oldest and the strongest witch of all of us. I'm surprised the coffee pots weren't exploding earlier when I told her about Derek. Lola is the second eldest; she's thirty-one. She's nice, but she's close to Molly. So, you have to be careful what you say around her sometimes because it could get back to Molly."

"Are you afraid of Molly or something?"

"No," laughed Violet. "She cares about us. Perhaps a little too much sometimes, but she can be a little controlling."

"What about the other two I haven't met?"

"Rosie and Lenore? They're both twenty-one. Still in undergrad, they go to the same school as us. I'm surprised you haven't seen them around. They can be kind of obnoxious together. But they're a tag team. They're kind of like spiritual twins. They were born at the same hospital, on the same day, same time. They're cool, but a little immature. And I swear they can read each other's minds, but they refuse to confirm it."

"And then there's Margaret?" asked Ellie.

"Yeah, Maggie. She's my best friend. I've known her since middle school. I wasn't born into a magical family, but Maggie's family taught me everything they know about witchcraft. She's... a little sensitive, but I care a lot about her. She was the one who convinced me to join the coven. She thought it would be better for both of us if a coven backed us. I guess she was right."

"It's nice, I guess," said Ellie. "You have built-in help if anything goes wrong."

"It's more annoying than anything else, but yeah, for times like these, it is nice." Violet drove silently for a few minutes. Ellie could tell she wanted to tell her something, but she bit her bottom lip as if to stop herself.

"Is something wrong?" asked Ellie.

"You believe me, right?" asked Violet.

"About what?"

"The reason I killed Derek was because he was going to kill my friend."

"I... I want to believe you. It's just, what's the alternative? That the man I love, that I've been with for almost three years, isn't who I thought he was? That he's been a monster this whole time? I don't know if I am ready to accept it yet, not with everything else going on." Ellie massaged her temple as a headache came on.

"Are you going to do it?"

"Do what?"

"Send him back."

Ellie stared out the window; the moonless night darkened the forest even more. "I haven't gotten there yet. What if there's a way to save him?"

"Why do you want to save him? After everything he's done? After everything he's done to you? He doesn't deserve a second chance, Ellie. But you deserve a second chance at life without that asshole attached to you."

"You have it all wrong. I was the one who couldn't let him go. And because of my selfishness, he continued killing. I don't think I deserve a second chance after what I've done."

"You didn't know he was a killer. Don't blame yourself for the information you didn't have."

Ellie tried to imagine what that second chance would look like. She could see herself finishing her degree, getting a job as a junior partner at a prestigious law firm. She saw herself happy, smiling, and in her bed; she saw River. His brown eyes were soft and sleepy in the morning light. His lips kissed her neck, where

Derek's hands had once been. It was tempting and beautiful, but doubt clouded her mind. The vision wasn't hers to keep.

Violet was about to say something else when a scraping sound, like metal rubbing against metal, emanated from the car. "What was that?" asked Violet. One, two, three loud bangs followed.

"It's coming from the trunk!" yelled Ellie. The trunk flew open, and Violet hit the brakes, her car coming to a grinding halt. The wheels made a high-pitched skidding noise across the pavement, and River's car did the same behind them.

"Is he still around?" asked Violet. The expanse of trees beyond the street was too dark for Ellie to see anything at all. If she had to guess, Derek had run away before the car stopped.

They stepped out and surveyed the damage to Violet's trunk. River joined them, his eyes wide. Three deep dents lined the inside of her trunk.

"Are you guys alright?" asked River.

"We're fine, and my car is mostly fine," said Violet.

"Should we go out to look for him?" asked Ellie.

"You guys didn't see it, but I've never seen anyone run that fast before. I don't think it's possible to catch him on foot."

"Then we keep going," said Violet. "They'll get worried if we delay any longer."

"Are you sure?" asked River.

"He could be out there killing more people," said Ellie.

"Unless you two are some sort of Olympic runners, there's no way that we're going to catch him! We keep going."

With that, Violet and Ellie got back into the car. Violet started driving faster towards their destination, and Ellie's headache got worse. Looking into the woods, she thought she saw red eyes peering from the darkness. They were being followed, but Ellie got the sense that it wasn't Derek.

Chapter Twenty-Four

As River pulled into the driveway, he couldn't help but think that if a witch wanted to hide, she could have picked a less conspicuous house. The home was Victorian, with high arches and painted midnight blue. The stained-glass windowpanes depicted roses growing from wild vines, and the wide turret's shadow loomed over the lawn. It stood out among the renovated modern houses around it. He had only been in this magical world for a short while, but if he had to guess which home belonged to a witch, it would be this one.

River got out of the car and followed Violet and Ellie to the front door. He helped them carry the box of stuff they had brought from the apartment. They knocked on the door, and River did a double take when Molly appeared on the other side. She looked surprised too as her eyes fell upon Violet in an accusatory manner. She shuffled them through the door and closed it behind them.

"Listen, before you get mad," Violet began.

"What is he doing here?" asked Molly.

"They're a package deal now. Honestly, River's not the biggest problem here. The boyfriend killed someone and left the body in Ellie's apartment."

"What?"

"We tied him up, and we were bringing him here, but he escaped."

"You weren't supposed to bring the boyfriend."

"I know, but we thought it was better to have him than to have him loose somewhere killing more people."

"But you lost him anyway, and in the meantime, lost us time."

"Molly, he's gotten incredibly fast. The bastard," said Violet.

River waited for the conversation to turn back to his intrusion and busied himself by looking around. He realized Molly's home was never meant for his eyes. Molly didn't hide her witchcraft in her own home. Pentagrams decorated the walls, feathers hung from the chandelier, and from the foyer he saw into the kitchen where jars of herbs sat on shelves on the wall. He hoped she would never get raided.

Molly walked them into the kitchen, and two people greeted them. Molly introduced the redhead to him as Margaret, while the second woman, who was tall and statuesque with purple hair down to her shoulders, was Lola.

"Where's Rosie and Lenore?" asked Violet.

"Rosie's out of town, but she's on her way back. And no one knows where Lenore is right now." If this were a cause for concern, nobody seemed that worried. River scanned their faces, wondering if any of them were anxious that she was Derek's next victim. Lola, on catching his eyes, smiled.

"She'll show up right on time. She always does." Her voice had a melody. A lyrical lilt in her Mexican accent that set River's nerves at ease. "You have the book?" she asked Ellie.

"Yes," said Ellie, opening the box that they had brought along. She pulled out an old, worn book. Lola ran her hands across the cover, brushing off something River couldn't see. She opened the book, letting her fingers glide over each page as she flipped through it.

"How many spells did you write?" asked Lola.

"None," said Ellie. "My mom wrote most of the spells. See," she pointed out the handwriting on two different pages. "My grandmother wrote some, as well as my great-grandmother, but my mom was the one who was into filling the book." Ellie's voice broke a little as she spoke. "I don't cast that often."

"You must still be a pretty powerful witch to cast a resurrection spell," said Lola. "Few people can bring back the dead by themselves."

"I don't think the spell was very successful," said Ellie as she placed a hand on her forehead and massaged her temple.

River followed her with his eyes, studying her every move. She fascinated him, and every little movement transfixed him. Her hair fell over her face as she bent down to peer through the book. She pushed it back behind her ear, and River wanted to do that for her. He noticed her long, slender fingers leafing through the book and wanted to kiss them.

In his dreams, he never needed to get to know her. The Ellie of his dreams knew him, his past, his present, and his future. She was as familiar to him as his childhood friends or his family. Dream Ellie was sweet, but mischievous. Sensitive and caring, yet selfish. She kissed him deeply and giggled into his chest as they lay together. He couldn't help but compare the flesh and blood Ellie to her dream counterpart. They were the same person; he reminded himself, but the real woman now stood before him, almost a stranger.

What I would have given not to have blurted out the future to her at our second meeting. We could have had more time.

He didn't know where the notion came from. Or why the idea made his heart plunge in his chest. Their time was up. He couldn't stop the next events from coming.

He returned his attention to Ellie. If he could focus on her, the rest would be fine. Yet, he got the creeping sensation of someone watching him. He turned to Violet's gray eyes, drilling into him. When he looked up, meeting her eyes, she looked away and busied herself with another book in front of her. He looked away and saw Molly staring at him. She didn't look away when their eyes met. He grew hot and walked towards her. He was an interloper; his presence here was putting Molly and everyone else on edge.

River had never had the slightest inkling of a suspicion that Molly might be a witch. She was good at hiding her witchcraft, and River wondered how many witches he had encountered in his life. If Molly was a witch, anyone was fair game. Hell, maybe Brian played up his hatred of witches to hide his own dark secret?

Molly said nothing as he approached, but he cleared his throat as if to say something. Yet, nothing came to mind. He wanted to apologize for inviting himself along, but he wasn't sorry about that. He was glad he had come. He wanted to admonish her for not telling him her secret. For thinking that he would be one of those terrible people that would turn her in, but she had every right not to tell him anything.

He settled for, "You have a lovely house."

"River," she started, but River whipped around.

As bile surged up his throat, his feet were unsteady beneath him, like standing on a boat in choppy waters. His temples hammered against his skull. River turned towards Ellie and saw her waver on her feet. He rushed to her and caught her in his arms as she stumbled, her body crashing into his. He was aware of people speaking, but he couldn't register what anyone said. Ellie lay motionless in his arms, but her breathing was steady. He called out her name to no answer.

"Lay her down." A hand pushed on his shoulder, and he turned to find Molly leading him to the living room. He laid her on the couch, and the others soon gathered around her.

"Maybe she's just exhausted," suggested Violet.

"Wait," River said. He pulled his hand from beneath her arm and raised it for them to see. It was sticky and red with her blood. Violet pulled up her stained sleeve, exposing the cut on her arm.

"When did she get hurt?" asked River.

"She wasn't. Derek didn't attack before you got there." Violet opened Ellie's eyelids. "Unless…"

"What?" asked River.

"I attacked Derek. I cut his left arm with a knife." She spoke only to Molly, and River grew frustrated. He didn't understand what she meant. "And River hit him over the head."

"Of course…" said Molly. She rushed out before coming back with a gauze and rubbing alcohol in her hands.

"What's going on?" asked River.

"Everything that happens to him, happens to her too," said Molly slowly, as if she was still mulling the idea over in her mind. She cleaned out the cut with a cotton ball.

"But it's delayed," said Violet. "And it's not as severe. At least I don't think it is. Derek's injury was much worse than this. She must be feeling the effects that Derek had when River hit him over the head with a lamp."

"Are you saying that everything that happens to him physically happens to her as well?" asked River, finally catching on. "Should we take her to a hospital?"

Molly leaned down and, like Violet, opened Ellie's eyelid. Satisfied with what she saw, she replied, "No need. She'll sleep it off." She finished wrapping Ellie's arm in gauze and motioned to River. "Follow me," she instructed.

River lifted Ellie and maneuvered around the others, following Molly through her house. They climbed the stairs to the second story and entered the first room across the stairs. River placed Ellie on the bed, as Molly went over to the window and pulled the thick velvet curtains closed. River moved the hair from her still face, letting his fingers linger on her cheek.

His nerves hadn't stilled since they'd left the kitchen. What did they mean by everything that happened to Derek happened to her? Were Derek and Ellie connected the same way River was with her?

"Hey," Molly said, moving closer to him. She placed a hand on his shoulder and motioned with her head for him to follow her out.

"I'm staying."

"She won't wake up for a couple of hours, and I need to talk to you."

He wanted to refuse, but he was in her house. Selfishly, he wanted to be near Ellie, but he knew he couldn't keep Molly away.

River followed her to the kitchen. As he entered, Lola, Margaret, and Violet turned to stare at him. The mood had shifted now that he was alone with them, without Ellie. Lola and Violet stared at him with an intensity as if their eyes could x-ray him. Molly offered no comfort as she walked over to the teakettle and poured boiling water into a blue mug. She stirred it, looking out the window, and River didn't understand why she had brought him downstairs just to ignore him.

As if hearing his thoughts, she turned and smiled. The smile had no warmth. It was a warning. She walked to where he stood and placed the hot tea in front of him.

"I want to trust you, River."

"You can trust me." He placed his hands around the mug. The heat warmed his freezing hands.

"If we're found out, you know what could happen to us," said Molly.

"Prison," said Margaret.

"If we're lucky," scoffed Violet.

"I would never expose you guys," River reassured them. "I hate these stupid laws, too."

"How were you dragged into this?" asked Molly.

River's tongue dried in his mouth. When he swallowed, it felt like sandpaper rubbing together. He couldn't explain it, but the drink in front of him looked enticing. He brought the mug to his face, the smell of the herbs intoxicating. The tea warmed his throat, but mid-gulp, a strange sensation took hold of him. Why was he so thirsty? He stopped drinking and glanced at Molly, who seemed to be waiting for him to speak.

"About four weeks ago, a body went missing from the morgue." He told her everything. Explaining the missing dead body and seeing him the next day. His need to keep Ellie safe, although he hadn't known why at first. Their conversations at school and his ill-timed warning. It flowed out, and River was only half-aware sometimes of what he said. It was an off sensation and, in some ways, freeing. How many secrets had he kept for a lifetime? How often would he get the chance to be as honest as he was being now?

"And what of Ellie?" asked Molly. "What's she to you?"

"I don't know, but there is a... pull. I want her, but it's not really a want; it's a need. She's my happiness. I'm not sure why." He stopped himself from continuing, but the words piled on his tongue, wanting to spill out again without his permission.

"Perhaps they are soulmates," said Lola. She looked up from Ellie's book, smiling. Her interruption stopped River's flow and his thoughts caught up with his mouth. He hadn't meant to say all that.

"Please," scoffed Molly.

"Perhaps it's because she is in danger? That could explain why the feelings are so strong," continued Lola.

"It's more than that," the words slipped out faster than River could stop them. He covered his mouth with his palm, his panic rising.

"What do you mean?" asked Molly.

His fingers uncurled of their own accord. No matter how hard River tried to fight it, his palm lifted from his face. "I... I have a gift."

The others, who had been busy with their respective duties, all stopped and observed him.

"What kind of gift?" asked Molly.

"I feel things. Like if something is off, I can tell. Or when something bad is going to happen, I know it before it happens."

"Is it normally when bad things happen?" asked Molly.

"Not always, but most of the time, yes. With Ellie, it's different. With her, it's a feeling like... like..."

"Like peace," Violet finished for him.

"Yes," River said softly. "Like peace."

"You're psychic then?" asked Molly.

"I mean, I don't have visions of the future."

"No, but you have clairsentience, and that's a psychic gift."

"What's clairsentience?"

"Clear feeling. It's an intuitive gift. You said you don't have visions, but you know the future in your own way. You can feel it here." She pushed two fingers into his abdomen. "And here," her hand traveled to his temple, tapping it lightly. "And here," her fingers moved from his forehead, down his face, and stopped at his heart. Molly took the mug from him and threw the rest of the tea into the sink.

"How long do the effects of your tea last?" he asked.

"A few hours," said Molly, "but I wouldn't leave the house if I were you, or you might spill all of your darkest secrets." Violet and Lola laughed, and while River should have been more annoyed, an exhausted chuckle escaped his lips.

"Are you done with me?" he asked.

"Yes, go back with your soulmate," said Molly.

He left the kitchen, not bothering to say goodbye to the others. His feet dragged. Each step up the staircase was like a hill for him to climb. When he reached Ellie's room, he stopped himself from entering. He lay back against the wall. His breathing labored to leave his lungs, and his heart beat furiously in his chest. Floral wallpaper lined the hallway. The intricate details of the dark-hued flowers made River's head swim. The more he concentrated on it, the more the flowers moved, as if a breeze existed in the wallpaper world, making the petals dance. Their fragrance wafted towards him, a mix of indolic white florals, causing his nausea to worsen. He closed his eyes, but the world still spun. He thought his legs would give out at any moment.

Was this a message from Molly? This wasn't a good high. He wanted to throw up. He didn't know what he had gotten himself into. He had been driving home a few hours ago, and now he was at his favorite barista's house, and she spiked his tea with God knows what.

Is it worth it?

He breathed in deeply, but the nausea wouldn't abate. He needed to lie down, so he opened the door and let himself into the room. His vision blurred, but Ellie's soft breathing somewhere in the room guided him. He let it anchor him, following it like a pinprick of light to pull him out of the trance. It seemed to work. His vision came back, and the nausea dissipated, albeit rather slowly. He kneeled beside her, finding his legs had no strength left. He let his fingers glide over her face, lingering in all the places he wanted to kiss. Her cheek, her jaw, the small hollow of her throat. Her skin grounded him, and for a moment, his head stopped swimming. There was something here, something in touching her that brought him back.

River wanted to stay next to her and keep his hand on hers. He thought it strange just to sleep next to her. But he wanted to; he wanted nothing more. He noticed the desk chair on the other side of the room, and he used the last of his strength to carry it next to Ellie's side. His hands found hers in the dark. Her skin was soft against his own chemically chapped skin.

His clairsentience, as Molly called it, that's what brought him here, and as he bent down to kiss her forehead, he knew he couldn't fight it. He didn't want to fight it. The voice in his head — the one he had often listened to that kept him safe in the past — was silent. Before it would have told him to run, to wait, to slow down, to think things through. Anything else instead of what he did now.

He was moving fast. It terrified him. It made his heart plunge and his stomach feel sick. But above all else, it gave him purpose.

Chapter Twenty-Five

Ellie could remember her nightmares most nights. They were often the same, involving a faceless villain whose fingers tried to snatch at the hem of her skirt. Some nights, she recognized who the villain was. Even if they revealed a blank face where there should have been eyes, a nose and a mouth, their familiar energy flooded around her. They were a dark swell that overpowered all her senses and left her gasping for air.

This night, her dreams revolved around Derek. His hands had turned to claws, and unlike previous villains, his hands touched her. The claws wrapped around her neck, as they had the previous night, but this time, his claws pierced through her skin. The more she fought, the deeper they buried into her flesh. She would die here.

As the dream unfolded, it changed almost as suddenly as it had started. The claws retracted from her neck, and she became fearful of her blood gushing out, but it didn't. Her hands floated to her neck, and they encountered uninjured skin. She turned around, and Derek was gone.

Ellie awoke then, her eyes adjusting to the darkness. She didn't recognize the room she was in, but to her side, she found River sleeping. His head rested on the bed while the rest of his body sat twisted in a chair. He cradled her hand in his. His fingers were slack but warm. She got the sense that if she pulled her hand away, his fingers would close like a trap.

She didn't want to wake him, but she indulged in the feel of his skin on hers. *What is this?* She wondered as the tingling sensation crept up her arm and spread a heavenly warmth in her chest. Whatever it was, it felt right.

Ellie remembered her handful of relationships. Some lasted; some didn't. She clung to each one tightly, praying that this time, with this man, she would be enough. That they would stay where others had left. Ellie thought that if she were perfect, had no problems, and made their lives easier, they would realize how worthwhile she was. She didn't fight with them when issues inevitably arose. She swallowed each problem and stuffed away any feelings of resentment that bubbled up within her heart. No, she would let it slide, let the worry extinguish, for this was love. And love was sacrifice.

Now, she had no clue what to think. This was a man who knew nothing about her, not really, anyway. All he knew were her issues, how flawed and messy she was. How pathetic she felt now, having to ask for help from a coven for the problems she started. She was nothing but a burden. Yet, this man seemed intent on carrying all her burdens, no matter how dangerous they were.

Leave it to me to find him when I've completely fucked up my life, she thought.

Divine timing, as her mother had once explained, meant that everything happened exactly as it was supposed to, even the bad things. Ellie had thrown away the entire concept after her mother died. What could be divine about her death? Her mother abandoned her. Left her to fend for herself as the world they knew around them fell apart and she became the target of its hatred and ire. Divine timing had a sense of humor if she could have only met River after she resurrected Derek.

Ellie sat up, waking up River. He startled awake before realizing that it was only her. He smiled, stretching his arms above his head, and heat rushed to Ellie's cheeks as he smiled at her. How many times had they passed each other? How many missed opportunities? Ellie grew mad about it.

"How are you feeling?" asked River.

"A little sore." Ellie examined her bandaged upper arm. "What happened?"

"Molly said you're connected to your ex. So, whatever happens to him physically happens to you. Well, it's delayed, but you'll feel it all the same."

River's thumb traced the lines in her palm. A wave of warmth spread across her body with a single touch, making her shiver.

"Do you feel that too?" asked River, as if reading her mind.

"Yes."

"Is it normal for witches? For your kind?"

"I've never felt it before." It was the truth, and in saying it, it seemed to satisfy something in River.

"River?"

"Yes?"

"How old are you?" asked Ellie.

River laughed, not expecting that kind of question. "I'm twenty-nine."

"Where were you born?"

"Austin."

"Texas?"

"Yeah, I lived there until I was twenty-five."

"Why did you move up north?"

"For a girl," he said.

"It didn't last?"

"No, it didn't." His eyes were pensive, sadness emerging from them. "But I stayed here. I liked the break from the heat, and I had already settled into my work. I like it here. Although I wouldn't mind less snow."

"The snow has been hard for me to get used to, too."

"What about you?" asked River.

"Twenty-five, San Diego, law school." She didn't know what else to ask. It was strange, having to relay the perfunctory demographic information she would normally dole out on first dates. Had she never told him she grew up in California? Did she really not know what brought him to Massachusetts in the first place? They had skipped all the polite small talk, and yet he didn't feel like a stranger to her. Not at all.

River laughed, and asked, "Have you always wanted to be a lawyer?"

"Not really, but it feels safer being on this side of the law. If that makes sense."

Ellie's decision to go to law school solidified after she watched the first witch trial in a hundred and fifty years on television. She witnessed someone innocent getting framed for witchcraft, and it disgusted her. Like the witches of Salem, real witches knew how to hide. Like Salem, it was mostly women and marginalized people who were forced to parade in front of the judicial system for entertainment. They had caught, tried, and convicted a few real witches. Ellie could always tell who they were. They held their heads high. Some were defiant and pleaded guilty, admitting to their practice, not allowing a lengthy televised trial. They denied politicians, judges, and the media what they wanted most — a spectacle. Ellie could never have imagined being that brave.

"It's safer knowing that you could defend yourself if you got caught," said River.

"In some ways, yes. I know that there are a few avenues that I would have if I got caught, but I could stay safe this way. And maybe help others who aren't as lucky."

His fingers moved up her wrist, following her veins. He kept his hand on her wrist as his thumb stroked underneath her sleeve. She longed for his hands to explore further and to feel his touch against her skin. He seemed to savor every small part he could touch.

"The book of spells is your mother's?"

"From my mother's lineage."

"You told me earlier that she died. Was she caught? Being a witch, I mean."

There were many witches who never received their "fair" trial at court. Many once accused were hunted down, and found dead a few days later. The police had a hard time finding the killers, not that Ellie ever believed that they looked hard enough. It was hard to find witnesses to testify that they had seen anything at all.

"She died from cancer," said Ellie, her voice catching in her throat. Without even thinking, River moved closer and embraced her. Ellie melted in his arms, wondering how he knew that this was what she needed from him.

What was this magic? This magic that held them together. Ellie had never felt it before. She had long since stopped paying attention to these kinds of magical moments. The small, almost insignificant energies that would float from her fingertips. The coincidences and chance moments that to the mundane eye meant nothing. The repeated numbers, the red feathers that floated down from nowhere, and the simple act of being held by someone who loved you.

She had shut it all away after her mother died. Numbed herself to magic. She had told herself it was for protection, not to arouse suspicion. Yet now she wondered if she pushed it away because magic carried memories. Her mother's laughter. The feel of her plump arms when she gave hugs. The sweet gardenia perfume she wore. She endured her loneliness, and magic became a reminder of how lonely she could be. Here in River's arms, she was safe. In his arms, she felt loved.

Ellie pulled away first, but she kept her face close to his, wanting to savor the energy radiating out of him. She couldn't stay numb around him, even if she tried. He cupped her face, letting his thumb wipe away the tears that fell. His eyes searched her face, lingering on her lips, and Ellie knew he was asking for permission.

She leaned in and pressed her lips against his. She pulled back briefly before he pressed his lips against hers again. His need of her grew. His desperation was evident in his every move. Ellie responded in kind. She wanted him. She wanted him more than she realized she had wanted anyone before. As his tongue slipped into her mouth, a moan escaped from her throat. Ellie pressed her hands onto his chest, his muscles taut beneath her fingertips. This was better than the kiss at the morgue or in the alleyway. Sweeter, because she would let him keep this memory.

River pressed against Ellie, and her back met the bed. River's body pushed against hers. His hands ran up her legs, and a shiver ran through her. She reveled in his touch. The firm grip of his fingers on her thighs. The caress of his tongue in her mouth. His body was flush against hers. She melted into him. She wanted to be as close as possible to him. Her hands floated to his clothes, wanting to tear them away.

River answered her fervor with his own. There was nothing gentle in his kisses. Nothing gentle in the way his fingers clutched her body. He kissed her neck, her collarbone, her chest. He worked his way down, leaving kisses behind that burned against her skin.

His kisses stopped abruptly, and Ellie waited for his mouth to return to her skin. He lifted himself off her, and Ellie sat up, confused. River straightened his shirt, and Ellie watched as he tried to smooth the wrinkles from where she had gripped his collar. Suddenly, there came a knock on the door. River called for them to come in, and Molly opened the door.

"Good, you're awake. How are you feeling?"

"Fine," said Ellie. River's face paled. He grabbed his black cardigan off the floor and draped it over his shoulders.

Molly looked tired, her eyes lined with dark bags. Ellie felt guilty for depriving her of sleep.

"Great to hear. Come downstairs. We have a lot to go over with you."

Chapter Twenty-Six

River and Ellie followed Molly downstairs to her kitchen. The windows allowed the golden rays of morning sunlight to stream through. Lola and Violet were sitting at the table, mugs in hand and somber looks on their faces. River felt it then.

Bad news.

"What did guys find out?" asked River before Molly joined the others at the table. The others looked away, not meeting his accusatory gaze.

"We can't unbind your soul from his," said Molly. "Everything we've looked through has told us unbinding you guys would be almost impossible. Short of sacrificing you for him, which we will not do, we're short on options. But we think we've found a loophole. Whatever happens to him physically happens to you, but with a delay. How long before you started feeling the effects of what happened to your boyfriend?"

"I don't think I felt anything until the drive over here. My arm was itchy, and it ached a little. That might have been ten, fifteen minutes after Derek got hurt. My head started hurting in the car, too."

Violet, Lola, and Molly shared a meaningful glance with one another. The uncomfortable silence between them persisted, and with it, River's irritation and frustration grew.

"So," began Ellie, "if you were to kill him. How much time would we have to unbind me?" The realization dawned on her face as it did on his.

"There will be a delay," said Lola. "I'm just not sure how much, but we can use it if there's enough time."

"If it took ten minutes to feel it in the car, wouldn't we have ten minutes?" asked Violet.

"I don't know," said Molly.

"How much time do you think I'll have?" asked Ellie again.

"A few minutes, seconds if we're unlucky," replied Molly.

Molly's resolve was unwavering, and River looked at the others to gauge their reactions. They were all lost in their own thoughts, but he didn't detect any hesitation on their faces. When he faced Ellie, he realized there was no fear in her eyes. But he was scared. His heart hadn't stopped hammering since they'd come downstairs.

He knew it wouldn't work.

"So, what's the plan exactly?" he asked, finding the silence unbearable.

"We're working on the technicalities, but basically once we kill him, it'll take some time for Ellie's soul to follow. In that short time, your soul should be technically untethered until his wounds kill you, too. We can maybe unbind you then. But we'd maybe only have a few minutes to do it."

"There are a lot of maybes in your plan, Molly. It doesn't sound very solid to me," said River.

"It's magic, River," Molly snapped back at him. "There are no absolutes. Every person's magic is different. It's not an exact science. Ellie's mother's resurrection spell is like others, and yet there were elements in it I've never heard of. You may hate this, but a lot of this plan is going to be on the fly. I can't give you guarantees."

His stomach churned. "It's not going to work," he said.

"River," started Molly, her voice steady and serious. He clenched his hands to stop their trembling. "River, you can't be sure."

"I am sure, and you know I am. We have to find another way."

"I know you're worried." He hadn't even noticed Lola had stood up and moved closer to him. He jumped at her voice in his ear. "If we found another way, we would use it. This is all we have."

"There has to be."

His body grew cold. Every cell in his body screamed at him. His gift had never been this strong before. He was used to the subtle pushes and pulls within his body. The way it could make his head turn in the right direction or fill his head and heart with dread when he heard something that didn't ring true. But now, it had never affected him this way, where even his bones seemed to shake and bile rose in his throat. His gift yelled at him to do something, anything. To stop the coven from killing the one person who meant more to him than anyone else ever had.

He was going to lose her. The thought stuck, its tendrils infecting every other thought in his head. How was this fair?

Ellie's fingers found his and, for a moment, the thoughts pulled back. He looked into her eyes; the warmth in them staked him at his core. He couldn't lose her now, not when he had just gotten her.

The nausea finally seemed to catch up with him. With a heavy heart, he released her hand and went up the stairs to throw up.

Chapter Twenty-Seven

Ellie stayed rooted to the spot as her eyes followed River out of the room. She studied the women sitting at the table, their faces somber yet determined.

"It's your choice," said Molly.

"Is there really no other way?" asked Ellie.

"We've looked through every resource we have. This is as close as we can get to make sure you're not bound to him anymore," said Molly.

Ellie looked away from them, tears welling up in her eyes. Everything led up to this.

"How could I have been so stupid?"

All this time, with a degree under her belt and her acceptance into a prestigious law school, she really thought she had it all figured out. Her life laid out — law school, a future career, and a man she would marry. Why had she deluded herself into thinking he was her soulmate?

"You were scared, and you were alone. But we're not going to let you do this alone," said Lola.

Ellie knew Lola was trying to help her justify her decision. What led her to cast a spell so dangerous and consequential? Of course, if she had had all the information before, she wondered now whether she would have cast it. Observing their grief-stricken faces, Ellie saw that on some level, they understood her desperation. She didn't know them well, but from their faces alone, they must have had moments of grief, sadness, and loneliness. Were they wondering if they would have been as desperate as she? Would they have sacrificed everything, even their own lives, if it meant the person they loved would be with them for a second longer?

She couldn't do anything to change the past.

"You're not alone now," Lola insisted. "We'll figure out the way."

"It makes a difference," said Violet. "Having sisters and a coven to help you. I can't imagine the power you hold to resurrect someone by yourself. With all seven of us working to unbind your soul, there has to be some power there."

Ellie sat down on the nearest chair, as her legs couldn't hold her up anymore. Molly placed a mug filled with tea in front of her. Ellie cupped the mug, letting the heat ground her.

"And you're not alone anymore," said Molly.

"And I won't die alone," said Ellie softly. *Of course*, she thought. She couldn't have messed with the balance of nature without becoming a casualty of it. She wouldn't make it. That would be the consequence.

"You won't die alone," repeated Molly. She motioned for Ellie to drink, and as she did, a sense of calm rushed from her chest to her fingertips. Molly was a skillful witch, alright. "And this way, your soul won't follow to whatever dark place his soul will go to when we kill him. You'll be free."

"Is there a chance I live?" asked Ellie.

Her thoughts drifted to a vision in her mind. It flickered like a lightbulb about to give out. She saw River there, lying on a bed she didn't recognize, his back turned to her. Soft birdsong floated from outside her window. The sun was just beginning to peek through the blinds. Sunlight shone on his back, and her fingers brushed over a small mole. She let her fingers linger there. His steady breathing lulled her into sleep again, but she wanted to stay awake. If she fell asleep, she was sure she would never come back.

"There is always a chance," said Lola, snapping Ellie out of the daydream. "It may be down to luck."

They sat in silence for a moment. Ellie concentrated on the warmth of the mug, letting herself focus on that than her impending death. Death was not a stranger. She always met it in passing, brief reminders of the inevitable. Now it would come for her. Ellie had no choice; if there were a way to do this that would save her life, they would've found it by now. Perhaps making sure her soul wouldn't be bound to his in the afterlife would be enough.

"Ellie," said Molly after a moment. "Do you know where we can find Derek? We tried tracking him with a spell, but he's all over the place. By the time we get there, he's gone."

"He might be back at the apartment? I'm not sure. He hasn't exactly kept to his schedule for weeks."

"We need to find him. Margaret went to gather a few things we needed, and there is still the question about the dead body at your apartment."

Ellie had almost forgotten about that. Last night felt so far away now.

"There is a lot we need to prepare, but we'll take care of it," continued Molly.

"I need to talk to River," Ellie said. Molly nodded. Ellie stood up to leave before turning back to them. "Thank you. I don't know what I did to deserve your help, but I am grateful. I'll never be able to make it up to you."

"You don't have to deserve it or make it up to us," said Molly. "You are one of us. And in this world, we protect our own. No matter what." Molly's eyes shone with intensity, and she meant every word.

Ellie left, and as she walked up the stairs, each step heavier than the last, her chest tightened. She leaned against the floral dark green wallpaper.

She would die. There was no other way. Despite the immeasurable sadness that filled her in that moment, she found beneath it all was an undercurrent of resolve. She needed to be strong. She would have to get through this and get River through this as well.

Stealing whatever courage she found deep in her heart, she walked into the room she had slept in the night before. As she opened the door, she watched as River paced the small room. The thick velvet curtains were drawn back, and Ellie took stock of the room. A desk stood in the corner, piled with textbooks and paper. The closet door stood ajar, revealing a wardrobe of black clothing. This was someone's room, but perhaps Molly had meant to keep her close to the stairs.

River was too entrenched in his thoughts to notice her. She walked in, closing the door behind her and breaking whatever black hole River had been spiraling towards.

"It's not going to work," he said.

"It's all we have."

"There has to be another way."

"There isn't."

"I won't let them kill you," he said as he walked towards her. His hands cupped her face. He looked into her eyes, willing her to understand, but Ellie stayed firm.

"I'm not going to die," Ellie lied.

"You are."

"How do you know?" Ellie narrowed her eyes, her suspicion rising.

River knew nothing about magic. She didn't understand how he could be so sure. He let her go, but she marched back to him and grabbed him. She became intensely aware of him as her hands cupped his face in her palms. His blood rushed to his cheeks, warming her hands. His stubble pricked her fingertips. He was a breathing, living man. If only he had caught her sneaking Derek's body out of the morgue. If only he had stopped her. If only, if only, if only. She needed to let it go, but the pain of her mistakes and regrets ached every time she breathed.

His breathing calmed with her touch. Whatever this was, he felt it, too. She wondered how much heartbreak he would have saved her from if only they had met first. If somewhere, anywhere, they could have bumped into each other. Ellie tried to stop thinking about it. It wasn't helpful. She couldn't change anything anymore. They had this moment, and perhaps the rest of the day. She wouldn't waste it ruminating on a past that she had no control over anymore. She wouldn't waste it on her regrets.

River's breathing had settled, and his arms wrapped around her waist.

"How do you know the plan isn't going to work?" she asked.

River's hands fell away from her body, and he walked away from her towards the window. Ellie followed, finding it hard to stand without his steadying energy. She looked out the window with River, and they were silent as they watched Violet pull out of the driveway. She waited anxiously for the truth. It was on the tip of his tongue.

"I know the plan won't work the same way I knew where your apartment was and that you needed help last night. The same way I knew Molly was going to knock on the door this morning before she did. It's how I knew your boyfriend was going to die before he did." He looked at her after this confession. She held her breath, and he continued. "The same way I know that you and I are meant for each other. I have a gift, Ellie. Molly called it clairesen-something. Clear knowing."

"Clairsentience?"

"That's it. I've had this gift for as long as I can remember. I don't tell many people about it, and since the trials, I've been afraid to tell anyone in case I'm reported. I've had to hide it, Ellie, the same way you've had to hide your witchcraft."

He sat on the bed, his body slumped and exhausted. His eyes bore into hers, wanting to make sure that she understood. It all clicked for her. He had no control over any of this, just as she had little control over her feelings for him. They were being pulled together by an unknowable force, like a stitch between fabrics. Something pulled the string taut between them, bringing them closer and closer. They couldn't fight it, and Ellie didn't want to fight it.

She held his hand again, letting herself feel the magic between them. Like an electric current, it flowed from him to her. She should have known; she should have paid attention to it sooner. He didn't feel like Derek, or any of her exes before him. The energy between them was like a soothing breeze on a hot summer day. Familiar, peaceful, and like home.

"There is something else. You asked me why I moved up north. I told you it was for a girl. I was with someone for four years. Her name was Natalie. She and I..." his voice cracked. "I loved her and trusted her, so I told her about my gift, but she didn't always believe me when I told her about what I knew. For her, it was something evil. Dangerous even. Sometimes I think she was afraid of it, like it was an omen. She thought I had control over it. And when I would tell her things that were about to happen, she accused me of doing it to freak her out or scare her. Sometimes she wanted to prove to me that I was wrong. I was normal; I had no gift. It was easier for her to love me if this gift was in my head or not real. She couldn't love someone who was different like that.

"So, I held back from telling her. I didn't want to cause a fight or make her uncomfortable, so I didn't tell her. That was fine for a few years until one day I felt it. She was going to die. It was so strong it made me sick. Even if I tried to push it away or ignore it, it was too powerful. I begged her to stay home. But she insisted she wanted to go to work. I told her about my feeling. Her face…" he broke off again. Ellie didn't want him to continue. She could see how much pain it caused him.

"She told me that everything was fine. She was mad at me, disgusted almost, as if I was making a joke to keep her at home. No matter how much I begged, she left."

His hands shook, and Ellie wanted to take away his memories. The same way she had before. She wanted to erase Natalie from him, erase all his pain, but she remembered the photo in his office. The photo of him and a woman with long straight blond hair. With her arms around his waist, she remembered the pang of jealousy she'd felt looking at that photo. She couldn't protect him from the pain in his past, but she wanted to protect him from more.

He wasn't wrong about the plan not working, but Ellie didn't want to let him know she was ready to die. She realized he would never let her go. He would fight for her until the end. Ellie's heart sank at the thought of him being in the same situation once more.

"I believe you, River."

He snapped to look at her. "You do?"

"Yes."

"You believe me," he repeated it as if he couldn't believe it.

"Yes, but we don't have another option."

"There has to be another way. I can't lose you."

He kissed her, and if Ellie thought his previous kisses were laced with hunger, nothing compared to this agony. She responded in kind, her own need a response to his. She pulled him in closer. Ellie wanted to feel more of him. She pressed her body against his, and his hands gripped her harder, as if she would disappear into smoke if he didn't.

Ellie pulled away first, her head and body spinning. She rested her head in the crook of his neck. She whispered in his ear, "What does your clairsentience say about me?"

"It's never been this strong before. I thought I was going crazy." A small laugh escaped his lips.

Ellie kissed his neck, and he shuddered beneath her. His hands grasped the nape of her neck, pulling her to face him.

"Everything that's happened. Everything that I've been doing has been leading me to you," he said. "I couldn't let what happened to Natalie happen to you. I've tried so hard to help who I can when I can. But I've had this growing fear in me for the past couple of weeks. I was afraid that I'd be too late. That no matter how hard I tried, I couldn't save you."

"I'm here now," she said, letting her hands caress his arms, his back. Taking in as much as she could. She pushed the thought of her death away. She was here now. That's all that mattered.

"But for how long?" said River.

"For as long as I can," she said honestly.

"It's not enough," he said.

She understood what he meant; she would have loved a lifetime of this.

"Are you scared?" she asked.

"Yes."

"I'm scared too," she admitted.

"Do you want me to stop?"

"No," said Ellie.

At that, River's arms wrapped around her waist as he shifted forward. Her back hit the bed, and when she pulled her face away from River's neck, his lips found hers. His tongue parted her lips, and his soft tongue danced with hers. She was keenly aware of his body. Every part of him that touched her seemed to burn. When she pushed her hips up and against him, his groan made her smile. He needed her as much as she needed him.

River pulled his lips away from hers, and she whimpered. He smirked, kissing her neck.

"I'm sorry," he said. "Did you want me to keep kissing you?" She nodded as his hands started traveling downwards. His fingers popped open the buttons on her jeans. "I'll kiss you again, but there's something else that I want to kiss first." Her heart hammered against her chest as he started kissing his way down.

He greedily helped her out of each article of clothing on the way down. She arched her back as she took off her shirt. He kissed her breasts as she arched. His hand fisted her bra out of the way. His lips licked her nipple, and he gingerly sucked on it. Ellie's breath hitched in her throat.

River continued his descent, and Ellie lifted her hips to help him take off her jeans and her underwear along with it. River kissed her inner thighs, leaving a trail of heat leading to her core.

His tongue circled her clit, and her breath came in quick gasps. He savored her. His tongue, slow at first, quickened as her pleasure rose. His hand rested on her stomach, stopping her twitches, and stopping her from lifting her hips to grind against him. She boxed him in with her thighs, willing him to stay there and never leave.

He didn't seem to want to leave anyway. He held her thighs in place, looping his arm around the right one. Ellie shut her eyes; everything was too much suddenly. The light streaming from the windows, the sounds of passing cars, and the smallest speck of dust on her skin felt too heavy. Her release was sudden. Her legs shaking on either side of River's head.

He lifted himself off slowly, kissing up her stomach. He didn't spend too much time on her breasts as he wanted to kiss her. She tasted herself on his lips.

He waited for her breathing to slow down to normal, kissing her all the while and letting his hands rove her body. His hands traveled down again, and he slipped a finger between her lips, parting them once again.

She couldn't speak. She trembled as his fingers entered her. He was dragging this out. How much time did they have? But River stopped any thoughts of the end bubbling up in her mind. He kissed her as if they had all the time in the world. He reveled in her, taking her in, letting himself explore every part of her.

His fingers curved inside her, and he stroked her slowly. It was too much. She was already on the edge again. She needed him. Badly.

"In time," he crooned against her ear.

"What?" she asked. Had she said the last part out loud?

"I know what you want," he said.

He dragged his fingers out and lifted himself directly on top of her. She placed her hands on either side of his face as he lowered himself down. He was careful not to put his entire weight on her. His gentleness made her jittery. Her need was too great for gentle.

He rubbed his cock against her entrance, letting it get slick with her wetness. The head of his cock rubbed her clit, sending shocks through her body. She moaned as he entered her slowly. His cock was snug within her, stretching her out. He moaned, cursing into the crook of her neck. He kissed her neck as he moved, a kiss planted after every thrust.

She was close, and by the groans that escaped River's lips, she knew he was close too. The air was stiflingly hot, and each breath brought on an onslaught of kisses and thrusts that left her gasping for more.

River's breath was short too, muttering a mixture of 'beautiful', 'perfect', and 'fuck' after every thrust.

When she thought she couldn't take it, when she thought she would burst, he reached down and rubbed her clit. She came with a quivering force that made her claw at River's back. Her back arched, but he pushed her down, kissing her all the while. He came soon after, his lips finally breaking away from hers.

CHAPTER TWENTY-EIGHT

River didn't want to stop touching any part of Ellie that he could get a hold of. The feeble autumnal light cast shadows against her lovely brown skin. His fingers stroked her hips, outlining the shadows from the blinds. He pinched a roll of fat. She hissed and laughed at the pain, pushing away his hand.

"You're perfect," he murmured against her neck. He would never exaggerate. Every part of her seemed made for him. Her warmth, her softness, the moles on her chest. Was it magic? His gift? Something made their physical connection stronger than anything River had ever felt. His mind could barely focus on anything else.

His dreams, where he had spent his nights sleeping with her, kissing her, relishing every part of her, were grossly unsatisfying compared to the real thing. Her sleepy eyes fought to stay open. She sighed with satisfaction as his thumb massaged her nipple.

Ellie giggled to herself, her laughter shaking her body enough to move him.

"What's so funny?" he asked.

"Nothing," but she laughed harder, and River lifted his head from her chest.

"Tell me," he chuckled.

"You won't find it funny."

"Try me."

"I was thinking about how it took me bringing someone back from the dead to have the best sex of my life. If I had known that sooner, I would probably have been resurrecting people all the time." Her laughter was infectious, and River laughed too. Her laughter was the center he had always hoped for. He wanted to make her laugh for a lifetime.

"I liked that you made noise," she laughed harder.

"Did he not make noise?" asked River. He didn't want to say Derek's name. He didn't want to talk about him at all. The thought that he had Ellie for years, years that River might never have brought the future into their bed. Or rather, the lack of it. River wanted to keep it away. The longer he kissed her and held her, the further away it seemed.

"He... grunted once. But he was always silent. Other guys have been quiet before, too. It sometimes made me think I was doing a bad job or something."

"They were fucking idiots," he said, kissing her. "Everything was perfect. You're perfect."

"I don't get why you keep saying that."

"Saying what?"

"That I'm perfect. After everything I've put you through. After everything I put everyone through. I am far from it, clearly."

"You are perfect to me. Even after all that you've done. It doesn't change how I feel about you. I wouldn't love you more if you had no problems. I would love you just the same."

"Love?" she said, staring at his hands.

"Love," he said. He ran his fingers along her neck.

Ellie shivered next to him. He loved the reaction he got from her. Every shudder, every hitched breath, and sound that escaped her lips made him more and more obsessed.

"I keep thinking," continued Ellie, in between his kisses. "How much of my life would have been different if I had just met you first?"

"I know," he said. He didn't want to think about it, but Ellie appeared determined to talk about it.

"You could have just approached me on the street or coffee shop, you know?" she said.

"I've never seen you before now, I swear. If I had, I would have approached you. I would have talked to you. I would have used one of my cheesy pickup lines."

"You have cheesy pickup lines?" She was getting breathless, pushing her hips against him.

"Yeah, a few."

"Is your boyfriend's dead? Date me instead, one of them?"

"That's the main one," he laughed.

Ellie laughed before sighing and pulling away from his lips. "My mother always told me that everything happens at the right time. Whether we like it or not, we weren't supposed to meet until now. As annoying and cruel as it is."

"Everything happens at the right time?"

"It's supposed to," she said.

"Because I wonder how many times we missed each other. How many times we might've walked by each other, or just been in the same building? How can it be that we're only meeting now?"

"I've been thinking about that, too. I wish I had an answer for you. I wish your clairsentience had led you to me sooner. I wish I had never met Derek, but had met you instead. You would have been much better for me."

"It's not fair."

Ellie's fingers brushed his hair back, and he leaned into her touch. Her eyes were sad, and she wanted to say something more, he could tell, but he grew fearful over what she would say. His heart dreaded her ending the small spell of the present. The only moment they had to push away the world.

"Let's run away," said River.

"What?"

"You and me. Let's get in my car and just leave. We can have more time and figure out how to actually unbind you from him. We'll figure it out, because all I know, Ellie, is that this feeling, this love, it's too good for it to just end. Life is too mean and fate too cruel if it's all to end before it's even started."

"River," she started. River placed his fingers over her lips.

"Don't say it," he said.

"How do you know what I am going to say?" she asked.

"I don't. All I know is how I feel when you say my name like that. It sounds like a goodbye, and I won't accept it. I'll never accept it. This was fast and sudden. I get that. Maybe it's not under the best circumstances; I'll give you that. But I won't give you up, not now, not ever."

Tears fell from Ellie's eyes, and River kissed them away. The saltiness passed from his lips and onto his tongue.

"I want that," she said. "I want a forever with you. I've never felt so sure about anyone as I do about you." River could sense the 'but' coming. "I made a mistake. And I won't ever be able to have that forever with you if I don't fix it. I was stupid for bringing Derek back when I should've let him go."

"Stop that," he said. "You're not stupid." River wondered how many times Derek had demeaned her, talked down to her, told her she was stupid or crazy. He wanted to hurt Derek. The asshole deserved a fate worse than death.

"River, I can't leave this mess behind. Like it or not, I have to fix it. Who knows how many more people Derek might kill, all because of me?"

"Then I must be a selfish bastard because I don't care what happens to anyone else. I only care about what happens to you."

He meant it too, but Ellie was different. He understood that now. She was braver than he ever was, or ever could be. She didn't run away. River ran away. He'd run all his life from his gift, and away from the supernatural knowledge he could've used to save others. He convinced himself it was all to protect himself, but fear ruled him. Fear that one day his gift would get him killed. He put his safety and life before others, and he realized Ellie would sacrifice her own.

She cried in his arms, and he held her closer. He brushed her hair back from her face. His eyes stung with the tears he held back. There was nothing he could say that would make it better. She calmed down in his arms, her face against the crook of his neck. He waited until her breathing returned to normal to continue.

"We will have our forever. You'll see. I don't know how, but we will," he whispered. "I can see it now. I couldn't before. But everything I've done, every step I took, was leading me to you. My gift has taken many things from me, things I haven't even told you about yet. But there's time for that. You may not believe it, but there is still time. I won't take my gift for granted anymore. It led me to you, and I will be forever grateful for that. But I won't let it take you."

He waited for her to say something, but she stayed quiet. River figured she was letting it sink in, but her breathing came steady and heavy. She had fallen asleep. River chuckled to himself.

He brushed her hair back with his fingers and breathed in her scent. A heady, woody vanilla engulfed him. It smelled so familiar, and as he drifted off, he realized he had smelled it in his office the day before.

River dreamed of love. He had been dreaming of love for weeks now, but that love had been frantic, confused, and laced with death. This love was warm, calm, wrapping them safely together. He sat on a porch he had never seen, and Ellie sat next to him on the swing. Her dark hair rolled down in waves on either side of her neck, and it surprised him how much longer it was. They waited out the thunderstorm. The air grew thick with moisture, and the wind picked up speed. She reached for him, and he wrapped his arms around her.

The storm would come, but River wasn't afraid of it. The defiance was easy. As if the decision had never had to be mulled over in his mind. It was easy because it was right. If he held on to Ellie, onto this feeling, they would survive this storm.

River heard a scream. He looked at Ellie, meeting her confused eyes. He shot up from bed and turned to see a girl with shoulder-length black hair and an all-black outfit standing in the doorway.

"What are you doing in my room? In my bed!" she screamed.

River and Ellie scrambled off the bed, trying to hide their naked bodies as best as they could. River stumbled, his eyes blurry from sleep.

"I'm sorry," called Ellie from behind the bed, as she desperately looked for her underwear. "I'm Ellie, by the way."

"Oh, so you're who I cut my trip short for. Who's this?" she pointed to River. "I thought your boyfriend was a monster."

"That's not my boyfriend," Ellie said.

"Hi, I'm River." He reached out a hand to shake hers, but she looked down at his hand and then back to his face with disgust. He felt judged by her perfectly manicured eyebrows.

"Rosie," she said without offering her hand. "Have you met everyone?" She directed the question to Ellie.

"Almost, I think we're missing Lenore."

"Don't worry about her. She'll show up. I'm going downstairs. I'll meet the two of you there. Also, if you two don't mind stripping the bed. I don't even want to touch my sheets." As she sauntered out, a nervous giggle escaped from Ellie's mouth.

River smiled as he walked over to where Ellie struggled to pull her jeans over her hips and kissed her. He thought better than to cross Rosie. He stripped the bed and carried the sheets downstairs.

"Where's the laundry?" he asked Rosie sheepishly. She pointed to the room by the back door. He started the wash cycle and returned to the kitchen.

Rosie caught Ellie up on the news she had heard since touching down at the airport.

"Molly says they still can't find Derek. I'm the best at tracking, and she said you had some personal items of his."

"Yeah, his hair is in that bag by the sink." Ellie pointed to the plastic bag. River noticed the faint blond hair in clumps and a comb. "I don't know how much good it'll do. They tried tracking him earlier, but they've had no luck."

"They did spells to track him," said Rosie. "I don't need a spell." She opened the bag and grabbed the hair.

"You can track him yourself?" asked Ellie.

"In my own way. It doesn't always work exactly how I want it to. But sometimes I can track them. Other times, it's like I can climb into their heads. It's not a perfect system, which is why Molly tried tracking him the old-fashioned way. But I guess she's desperate enough to try me."

She closed her eyes, her fingers running through the hair. River looked at Ellie, but she looked as intrigued as he was. Perhaps this wasn't as normal in the witch world as he thought.

"What do you see?" asked Ellie.

"It's not so much about seeing. It always looks more abstract. I see colors; sometimes it's more of a silhouette, other times objects. I have to look around because it's not always so obvious."

River turned to Ellie. She listened intently, but none of it made sense to him. "So, what do you see?" he asked her again.

Rosie sighed, "Red. It's wet. Blood, I think."

Ellie turned to River, reaching out to hold his hand.

"There are a lot of leaves. He was in the forest. I can see a booth, like ring toss?"

"I don't think this is working," River whispered to Ellie. Molly had warned him that witchcraft wasn't an exact science. He knew that his own gift hardly followed prescribed rules most days, but nothing Rosie said made sense.

"He's moving," said Rosie. "I see blue. A door." Rosie's eyes snapped open. "Shit."

"What?" asked River.

Before River reacted, before anyone could move an inch, the front door of the house flew off its hinges. Derek stormed in, reaching the kitchen in a few quick strides. River forgot Derek could move so fast. Instinctively, he stood in front of Ellie.

Derek looked crazed. His eyes were red, and foam fell from the corners of his mouth. He looked as if he had been running all night, his clothes torn and dirty. He kept his gaze on Ellie. River wasn't sure if Derek even registered he was standing in front of her or that Rosie was in the room.

He walked closer to Ellie, and Rosie stood in front of River and Ellie.

"You get any closer and I'll kill you." She held a kitchen knife in her hand, pointed towards him. Derek didn't move forward, but River wondered if Molly had told Rosie that if she hurt him, she would hurt Ellie too. He didn't want Derek to have that information.

"You need to fix this, Ellie!" Derek yelled, spittle coming out of his mouth.

Rosie scowled as some of his spit landed on her. "You need to be more specific," she said. "We can kill you now, and everything would be fixed, wouldn't it?"

"These things were chasing me all night. They wouldn't leave me alone," Derek said, ignoring Rosie.

"What do they look like?" asked Ellie. Her voice held a note of surprise, but River was unsure what they were speaking about.

"They're like birds, but bigger. They fly, and when you get too close, they change..." his voice trailed off. Whatever these creatures were, Derek's experience with them left him shaken. Yet, apart from his clothes, Derek appeared otherwise unharmed.

"They're here for you," said Ellie. River wanted her to stop talking, not to draw attention to herself. "They're here to take you back."

"So, you sent them?"

"No, I didn't. I can't control them. They're here because I messed with the balance of nature by bringing you back. They're here to balance it again."

"And whose fault is that?" asked Derek. Ellie walked in front of both Rosie and River. Every sense he had rang in his body, telling him to stop her. Pull her back and hide her.

"Derek, I'm sorry. I shouldn't have brought you back. I loved you, and I should've let you go." Derek walked closer, and River had to stop himself from jumping forward and pushing Derek away. He couldn't hurt him, and that was unbearable.

"You know what pisses me off the most about you, Ellie?" His eyes bulged out of their sockets. "I should have killed you a long time ago, and I almost did. A few times, actually. But you know why I didn't? Because no one would look for you. And there is no fun in killing someone that nobody is going to miss."

River couldn't have stopped himself even if he'd tried. He lunged forward, punching Derek straight in the jaw. Derek stumbled backwards, and River stepped forward to shield Ellie from harm. As his blood rushed to his ears, Derek straightened himself right again and looked poised to attack back. River only realized then how much harm would come to Ellie if he fought him.

Derek didn't hold back. He pounced on River, dragging him to the floor. River dodged the first blow, but he didn't dodge the second. A splitting pain swelled in his jaw and lips. River pushed Derek off, shoving him towards the cupboards. River stood back up, heart racing.

Derek started towards him, his lips curled in a snarl, when he stopped. He turned towards the window. River looked at Ellie perplexed but found her and Rosie staring out the kitchen windows too. River looked out but saw nothing but the trees with their yellowed and red leaves.

He turned to ask Ellie what was going on when Rosie yelled, "Duck!"

River didn't have time to take her advice, and something threw him back against the jars of herbs. He slid down the wall. His back ached, but he wasn't paying attention to that. He looked up at the scene of chaos. There was something in the room. Derek fought off something as it clung to his back. Something pushed Rosie out of the way with such force that she hit the fridge. He tried to look for Ellie, but a warm softness brushed against his legs. When he looked down, he found nothing. The creatures, he realized. He couldn't see them, but they had to be here.

He pushed himself up, looking for Ellie. Desperation pulled him forward. He called for her, his voice getting lost in the confusion. For a moment, he thought he saw her, crouched by the stove. He started making his way there, but an invisible monster pushed him to the floor. River pushed against it, and he cried out as a sharp pain exploded on his leg. He watched in horror as three long gashes bloomed on his skin. His blood pooled quickly, making the floor beneath him slick.

"River?" Ellie's voice rang through the room. He had to get to her.

River stood up again, the pain in his leg not stopping him. He watched her fight against the monsters. Her arms flailed in front of her, pushing against something he wished he could see. He opened his mouth to call out to her, but another blow lifted him from the floor. The last thing he remembered was flying back towards the living room, before everything went black.

"Come on, River," a voice stretched through the ether. It wasn't the voice he wanted the hear. The voice he had only just begun to love and cherish as a melody that he would play over and over. "Wake up!" He only then realized someone slapping his face repeatedly.

He startled awake, his sore body groaning beneath him as he sat up straight. Molly snapped her hands back from him, taken aback by his sudden consciousness.

He looked around and counted the people in front of him in his head. Margaret, Violet and Rosie stood near him, with Molly making four. Lola walked up then, her eyebrows stitched in worry. Five. He heard footsteps to his left, and he turned around, hoping that they belonged to Ellie. A face he had not yet met appeared. She had lovely hazel eyes, and she twisted her brown hair in worry.

"Lenore," he croaked bitterly. Six.

She gave a half-hearted smile, but River read the concern in her eyes.

"Where's Ellie?" he asked.

"He took her," said Rosie, holding a kitchen towel to her bleeding head. "I tried to grab her, but those damned creatures stopped me."

River felt as if they tore his heart, bleeding and pulpy, from his chest.

Chapter Twenty-Nine

It all happened so fast that Ellie had no time to react. The creatures crashed through the windows. She turned to River but saw him thrown against the herb shelves. The jars burst around him, falling like confetti on the floor. She ran to him, but soft black feathers brushed against her side. The creature's full strength pushed her against the cabinets by the stove. Her back ached, and her feet slipped on something slippery when she tried to lift herself up. Someone grabbed her waist, helping her up. She turned, hoping to see River next to her. To her horror, it was Derek. His talons stabbed through her shirt and pierced her skin, pinning her to him. She thrashed and kicked, but his claws buried deeper into her flesh. A hot, searing pain on her leg distracted her from struggling against Derek as the creature's claws burrowed into her calf.

She screamed as Derek yanked her away, dragging the creature's claws down towards her ankle. Pain and dark spots clouded her vision until everything went dark.

Ellie woke up in her bed in her apartment. She was disoriented and confused as her eyes darted around her surroundings, expecting to see Derek looming in the corner.

Her room looked normal. Cleaned even. For a small moment, she thought perhaps she had dreamed it all. A nightmare, or a premonition perhaps. She could have stopped it before it began. Yet, the pain in her leg brought her back to reality. The wound was deep and untreated. She looked around for something to bind her throbbing leg and settled on a scarf in her drawer. It would have to do for now, but her hands shook from a mix of fear and pain. Her jaw ached as well, no doubt from the punch River threw at Derek.

She moved quickly and silently, trying to listen for any sound outside of her room that alerted her to Derek being nearby. She needed to contact the coven and fast, but her pockets were empty. Her phone might have fallen in the chaos. The coven would be worried, but above all, she knew River would be worried sick.

She pressed her ear against her bedroom door, but the only thing she could hear was her heartbeat and the blood in her body whooshing through her eardrums. She would have to take a chance. There was no time to waste.

She stepped out of the room, knowing where to step to not make a sound. Something she had picked up early in her relationship with Derek.

Outside her room, she sidestepped around the body of the dead woman. Ellie looked at her, bile rising. The woman's hair was caked with dried blood. Her dull eyes stared at the ceiling.

Her fingernails were torn off her nail beds. Ellie didn't want to think about what this woman's last moments were. What Ellie's own fate would have been if Derek had decided she was no longer worth keeping.

She needed to leave and rejoin the coven again. Her car was still in the parking lot. She just needed to get her keys. She hobbled towards the kitchen, finding not only her keys in the bowl where she normally kept them, but her phone on the counter as well. As she reached for it, a hand wrapped around her throat.

Derek pulled Ellie and slammed her back against the wall. She gasped, trying to get the oxygen back into her lungs. Derek's fingers wrapped tighter. He lifted her up so she could meet his eyes, and her toes scraped the floor. She clawed and scratched at his arm to make him let her go, but his hand squeezed her throat tighter. He held up his other hand, showing her the four talons where his fingers should have been.

"What's happening to me, Ellie?" He'd never sounded so desperate before. She'd never even seen him cry, but now the man behind the monster emerged. She realized she'd never seen it before, even when they were together. In his despair, he was finally vulnerable.

"You're turning into one of them," Ellie said with difficulty. Derek loosened his grip around her neck, his desperation so great that he wanted to hear what she said.

"Into what?"

"Into the creatures that attacked us."

"What?"

"Your soul — it's a reflection of who you are." Derek's eyes darkened. "And you're a monster."

He hated that, but Ellie didn't regret saying it. He grabbed her neck and flung her across the room. Ellie landed on the coffee table, collapsing it with her weight. Every muscle ached, and it became clear he didn't feel her pain the way she did his. He sauntered towards her, unfurling his talons. He was going to kill her in the home they shared. In the room where they used to laugh and cuddle. None of it mattered to him. She never mattered to him.

He lunged forward, and Ellie shut her eyes. The attack never came; instead, a crashing sound echoed through the room. She opened her eyes to find him sprawled on the floor across from her. Derek flipped over with a grunt and stood up, rage causing more spittle to fall from his mouth. He ran faster towards her, and shiny black feathers began to sprout on his arms. Derek hit something, although Ellie couldn't see what. He huffed; his voice sounded distorted, deeper. He outstretched his arm and pulled back his hand quickly, as if it burned.

"What is this?" he yelled at her. Ellie didn't know for sure, but she could guess. A protective force field, but she hadn't placed it.

"Don't come any closer," Ellie yelled back. "I shouldn't have brought you back, Derek. That's on me. But this," she pointed at his claws, "this is what you deserve."

"So brave now that you're protected. You're so pathetic," he spat back. More feathers grew on his body, pushing through his goose-bumped flesh. His face became pinched, morphing into the harsh, wrinkled features of a vulture. "I saw you the other night. Who is he? Huh? Already replaced me? Of course you have; you can't be alone. You've always been pathetic, Ellie. My biggest mistake was sparing your life. I should have killed you from the beginning. Is this what I deserve? After keeping you alive? After taking care of you? Putting up with your sensitive bullshit and baggage? Who would have you? No one but me! You know what you deserve? Exposure. You and your witchy friends. I wonder what'll happen when the town figures out witches walk among them?"

Ellie's stomach dropped. She was going to die. She had accepted it, but she didn't want the coven to be brought down because of her. They didn't deserve it, not after everything they had done to help her.

"You're not exactly looking very human right now, Derek. What do you think will happen when they see you?"

"They should witness what real witchcraft is! Not those people they show on TV. Those aren't real witches! They don't know what you guys are capable of! It's time the world knew, don't you think?" He smiled, and Ellie had never seen a more menacing sight.

"Derek," she said, but she had no idea how to stop him or how to plead her case to protect the others. She walked towards him, but the force field pushed her back a couple of steps.

"You can't move either," he nearly sang. He walked closer to Ellie, his shadow towering over her. He smirked, his dark eyes filled with mirth. "Goodbye, Ellie." He turned and walked out the door.

Ellie sat down, stunned. She pushed against the force field, but it wouldn't budge. A panic attack loomed in her chest. She had put the coven in danger. After everything they had done for her, this would be the end. She wouldn't allow it. Nobody else would get hurt because of her choices.

She brought her hand over the force field. It pushed against her hand like static electricity. Cold to her, but watching Derek earlier made her think it burned him. She let her hand hover. The cold was familiar, and then her hand bumped into something. A magical signature. One she had not felt for years.

Her mother's.

Ellie gasped, pulling her hand away. She cried as she placed her hand over it again. It was her mom. The signature held the same feeling as her mother's previous magical workings. The protections around their home growing up. The talisman her mother had enchanted to keep her safe. Even the items around their home, like books her mother had touched, bore her signature. Her mother was magical in every aspect of her life, and she never hid it. It stayed like fragrance on a scarf.

But Ellie found over time, one by one, the items in their home stopped feeling like her. First her books, then her makeup, then her clothes. The day her mother's spell book stopped feeling like her, Ellie placed it away in the box. Grief made her avoid the book and magic altogether.

She couldn't stop crying as she relished the energy. She needed the force field to go away so she could warn the others. Derek had left in a hurry, and she could see her phone lying on the floor a few feet away from her. Yet, she didn't want to pull her hand away. She didn't want to lose her mother again. She had forgotten the warmth, the sense of security, her love. She'd missed her love most of all. In the force field, her love surrounded her, the way her hugs had often done. She'd been alone for so long. Lonely and desperate enough to bring Derek back from the dead. Yet her mother was still here. She wasn't alone. She'd never been alone.

Ellie had very little time. Taking a deep breath, she stood, her hands outstretched. She felt her mother one last time. "Thank you," she whispered.

The force field fell instantly, and Ellie stepped out. The room was colder, and she wanted to cry out, but she had to be strong. She picked up her phone off the floor and sat on the couch, letting her leg rest.

She dialed Violet's number, the only number she had on her phone from the coven.

The phone rang once, and Violet answered.

"Ellie! Are you okay? Where are you?" she sounded frantic.

"I'm fine. I'm in my apartment. Derek's gone," Violet started talking, but Ellie stopped her. "Wait, we have bigger problems. Derek's trying to expose the coven."

"Do you know where he would go?" she asked.

"Somewhere public, maybe?"

"The fall festival," said a voice that Ellie didn't recognize.

"Can you meet us there?" asked Violet.

"Yes," Ellie hung up the phone. She found her car keys and limped out of her apartment.

Sitting in her car, she took a deep breath. She would protect the coven. No matter what was going to happen, she would not let the others fall because of her.

CHAPTER THIRTY

River ran through the fall festival, crushing dead leaves and litter beneath his feet. He ran towards every woman around Ellie's height with brown hair. He called for her, and the women near him turned around to stare at him, confused and annoyed.

He tried to will his gift. It had never worked that way before, but he was desperate. His gift had been fried ever since Derek took Ellie. Almost as if his ears were filled with cotton. When he tried to listen, when he begged for guidance, it came back muffled and jumbled.

The coven moved quickly after Ellie's phone call. Almost as if speaking telepathically, they gathered supplies and grabbed what they needed for a plan that River knew wouldn't work. They had run out of time, even if they could have found something else. It was too late.

He was numb after she was taken. The surrounding voices became muted. She had called. She was safe, but he wondered for how long.

He climbed into Violet's car along with Molly and Lola.

"So, what's the plan?" he asked Molly.

"Rosie, Lenore, and Margaret are going into the woods north of the festival. They'll set up everything we need for the spell to unbind Ellie's soul from Derek. We," she said, pointing to Lola, "are going to look for Derek. And Violet's going to cause a diversion. You're going to look for Ellie."

"What's the diversion going to be?"

"No clue," said Violet from the driver's seat, "but I'll figure it out once I'm there. You'll know when it happens."

"Any questions?" asked Molly.

"You haven't figured out a version of this spell where Ellie lives." It wasn't a question, just a fact. He wanted some hope to hold on to, something that would stop the horrible sinking sensation in his stomach.

"I wish." Molly's eyes were sincere, leaving River with no doubt that she meant it.

The fall festival brought what River thought was more than half the town. He had even spotted Brian and his family buying pretzels. If Derek wanted to expose the coven, he had picked the perfect location. It was cold, colder than any October that River could remember. People were underdressed and shivered against the brutal wind.

River couldn't concentrate long enough to let his gift lead him to Ellie. The impending spell preoccupied him, reminding him that Ellie wouldn't make it. A steady drip of dead, dead, dead, that he tried in vain to stop.

He took a deep breath, willing himself to find her. Remembering her perfume, the woody vanilla that clung to her hair. Reminding himself of the weight of her body against his, the moles on her chest, the way she looked at him as she came. The memories left him cold, hungry to taste, feel, and hold her again. She had been gone for a few hours, but it was too long for him. Somewhere in this crowd, she was looking for him, and he needed to find her.

He felt it then, a small pull at his torso. He whispered a soft 'thanks' to his gift and ran towards the feeling.

She stood leaning against a booth, her eyes scanning the crowd. The people passing her by avoided her. She had wrapped a scarf around her left leg, and blood seeped through the other side, painting the blue scarf a rust color. Derek hurt her.

He started running towards her when Derek appeared behind her. His eyes burned red, his clothes tattered and dirty. He stared at Ellie; his eyes murderous. River ran faster, and Ellie jumped when his hands grabbed hers.

"River," she said.

There was no time for a reunion. He pulled her away, and they ran. Ellie had trouble keeping up, her leg making her limp. River looked behind him, but Derek wasn't there anymore. He noticed a ring toss booth unattended, with an out for fifteen minutes sign on the counter. He helped Ellie climb over the booth, and he followed. They hid under the counter. The sound of laughter and shuffling feet passed by, but River paid no attention to it.

They had turned the game's lights on, and in the dim parti-colored light, River took stock of Ellie. River glanced down at the shredded skin on her leg, and although she had tried her best to cover her wound, in her haste, she hadn't done it well. His eyes lingered on the bruise on her jaw, and he hated himself for causing it.

"It doesn't hurt that badly," Ellie told him.

"You don't have to lie to me. I did that to you," he said, reaching out and caressing her jaw. She leaned into his touch.

"Did he hurt you?" he asked.

"He didn't have the chance," she said.

"Your leg—"

"That was the creature," she assured him. "Derek threw me across the room, but he couldn't do much else."

River's hands clenched into fists. Derek would never hurt her again. He would make sure of it.

"What's the plan?" asked Ellie.

"We wait for Violet to cause a distraction. When she does, we run into the woods. From there..." he didn't want to say it, but he didn't have to. River couldn't fight against any of it anymore. Ellie would never listen to him or resist it. He would surrender to the inevitable, no matter how painful.

Ellie said nothing; instead, she leaned in and kissed him. As if she sensed what he needed. He let her part his lips. He indulged in the warmth of her mouth, and he wanted her to stay there. To stay in this moment, where they could kiss and feel each other into oblivion.

She pulled away first, her breath unsteady. "River," she started.

"Don't do it."

"You didn't let me finish."

"You were going to say goodbye."

She didn't answer, but she didn't have to. Her sad eyes reflected the blue and red lights of the booth, and her hands shook in his. He leaned down to kiss them, wishing that he could steady them the way her touch steadied him. His lips crushed onto hers, and he gripped her tight. A certain desperation made her kisses hungrier and frantic. Her fingers dug into his face, pulling him in closer. If this was it, he never wanted to be anywhere else than here.

He realized only then that he would follow her. Wherever she went, whatever she did. It was not the influence of his gift, but his own volition. He would follow her to death of his own free will.

Boom!

The booth reverberated with the sound of an explosion that made River's ears ring. He heard screaming from the crowd and the sound of a horde of footsteps running. Ellie looked only at him. Her eyes didn't show fear, but her determination ran through them. They stood up and waited for the crowd of people to disperse, their screaming and scrambling feet the only noise left in the festival.

River helped Ellie out of the booth, and they started towards the forest. Ellie limped alongside him, doing her best to keep up.

Right before they reached the woods, another explosion shook the surrounding trees. If there was anyone left near the woods, they had run out, fleeing towards their cars. They encountered no one else.

The temperature seemed to drop twenty degrees once the thick trees concealed them completely. River shivered from the cold and held her closer. They didn't run anymore. Her leg wouldn't allow it. He didn't know how deep into the woods they needed to go, but they continued north. She held onto him, and she slowed down more and more as they walked. Finally, he stopped and reached around her, helping her into his arms. She rested her head on his shoulder, and he focused on her unsteady breath on his neck. Anything to keep his mind from venturing too far into the future.

The further they walked into the forest, the stronger the smell of smoke became. The sharp crack of burning wood grew louder. River walked only a few feet further, and the coven appeared before them.

All six women stood around the campfire, their backs to River and Ellie. River expected there to be chanting, or something more magical going on. He half-expected to see a cauldron on the fire, but they stood in silence, eyes closed.

As they drew nearer, he saw Derek lying by a tree, his arms and legs bound by rope. Ellie massaged her forearms, and River realized she could feel the tightness of the rope on her own skin. An invisible, scratchy rope reddened her arm.

Margaret was the first to open her eyes. Her hair reflected the bright flame, making her own red hair appear to dance like the fire. She walked towards them as the others soon came out of the trance they were in.

"What's next?" asked Ellie as Margaret approached. River helped Ellie down, his sinking stomach worsening.

Rosie walked forward, a cup in her hand. She gave it to Ellie and without instructing her to do so, Ellie drank from it. Molly followed. Her eyes seemed to glow, reflecting the orange flames. She handed Ellie a knife.

"You know what to do," said Molly.

River thought the knife looked old. Its handle was ivory white, the pommel encrusted with a blue stone. His heart hammered in his chest, but he didn't stop her. He couldn't stop any of them. As she limped towards Derek, he wanted to hold her back, to keep her against him and run. He caught Molly watching him. Was she making sure that he wouldn't stop her?

All of River's muscles tensed as Ellie drew nearer to Derek, the knife clutched in her right hand. Derek looked wild. Half of his body was covered in brown and black feathers. His face looked like a half-bird, half-human hybrid. His mouth jutted forward, hardened into a beak, and his eyes shone yellow. The pallid skin around his eyes wrinkled. Ellie stood over him, knife poised. Derek's eyes stayed fixed on hers. He wouldn't look at the knife.

Derek shifted to the left. River wanted to yell at Ellie to watch out, but it was too late. Derek swung his legs, knocking her down. He flexed, the muscles in his arms and legs snapping the thick rope. Ellie rolled over onto her side and struggled to stand as River ran towards them. He tackled Derek away from Ellie as screams from some of the coven members echoed behind him.

Derek was strong, stronger than any normal human should be. River's arms struggled to hold him down. Derek pushed himself up, rolling on top of him. River struggled against him for a moment before Derek's fist crashed into his cheek. He dodged the next punch, gripping Derek's elbow. He pushed his hips up, pushing Derek off him. River scrambled up, and Derek did the same. Derek ran at him first, and River dodged his talons.

River waited, his body posed defensively, as he tried to guess Derek's next move. Derek's eyes darted frantically before they settled on Ellie. River lunged forward again, knocking Derek against a tree. He struggled to hold him in place, but an intense, fiery pain distracted him. Derek's claws buried into his right forearm. River yelled, not moving even though this arm throbbed from the excruciating pain. He looked up to see Derek smiling. Exerting little strength, Derek pushed River off himself.

River fell and rolled through the dry pine needles and dirt. He rose again, and Derek laughed. River's anger grew. He wanted to punch him. Fight, but he couldn't. Derek stalked towards him, his claws extended. River noticed Ellie standing a few feet from them. She held the knife in her two hands, watching the unfolding fight. Without thinking, River ran towards Derek, pushing him back by his shoulders. Derek laughed until he didn't.

He let go of Derek's shoulders, and the monster peered down. His blood, a mixture of red and black, spurted out from him. The knife shone with his blood.

Ellie didn't hesitate and pulled the knife out with a grunt. The blood flowed quickly then, and Derek stumbled back, falling at her feet.

Whatever momentary relief River felt dissipated as red bloomed on Ellie's shirt. He caught her before she fell, cradling her head in the crook of his arm.

Wasn't she supposed to have minutes? It didn't matter now, and River looked at the others, trying to see if they were casting the spell. Their voices raised in unison, but he couldn't make out the words. He turned to them and grew frightened as Molly shook her head. Lenore and Violet's arms were shaking.

"What's happening?" he asked. He placed his shaky hands over Ellie's wound, hoping to stop the inevitable. His gift screamed at him. His soul tore itself in half. A part of him was leaving with her.

"Guys?" he asked again.

"His soul won't let her go," Margaret yelled near him.

"We can't separate them!" Violet yelled.

"She needs somewhere to go," yelled Rosie. "She's too far gone."

"To me!" yelled River. He was only half-aware of what he said, but only focused on her fluttering eyelids. "Bind her soul to mine!"

"We have to; there's not much time!" He wasn't sure who said it.

River didn't know where the sensation came from. He felt cold, as if he had plunged headfirst into a frozen lake. A heat followed next. So intense, he thought the campfire had somehow stretched towards him. A sharp pain soon followed in his abdomen. The same blood flower bloomed on his shirt, matching Ellie's. He pulled back her shirt. The blood flow slowed, and the skin closed around the wound. She healed, while his own pain grew.

Ellie's eyes opened, and the knot in his stomach finally loosened. Her eyes stayed fixed on his, their warmth as inviting as the sun in winter. River's tears fell on her face, and her hands went up to brush them away from his face. He choked out a laugh that sounded more like an exasperated cry. Derek was dead, and her soul wouldn't follow him.

He didn't notice the stain on his shirt growing bigger, or his own blood gushing out of the wound. As she smiled, his body became clammy and cold. The pain was too sharp to ignore. Then everything went black.

Chapter Thirty-One

"What's all this?" asked Ellie, as Scott placed two stacks of exhibits on her desk with an annoying plop.

"I need you to write cover letters for each of these exhibits," he said it slowly, as if she were dumb.

"Are you kidding? This will take all day. I have other work." She looked through the stack. The pages were out of order, too.

"This is more important." He left without another word, and Violet rolled her eyes.

"I'll take care of it," she told Ellie, grabbing one stack from her desk.

"But you have your own work!"

"Don't worry about it. Who needs sleep?" she shrugged. "Go, River is waiting."

Ellie hugged Violet and grabbed her backpack. She ran to her car and skimmed Molly's message.

River was awake. She didn't know if it was for a moment, or if he was still awake, but she didn't care. She drove to Molly's house, an almost daily occurrence for the past two weeks.

The aftermath was messy. Ellie and Violet had buried Derek's body deep in the woods. There was no way they could have left his body for the police to find. His final form was something between a vulture and a human. With long black feathers covering half his body and his face resembling more bird than man.

There was a finality to it for Ellie, his grave unmarked and plain. Hidden forever. Violet made sure of it as she placed a charm bag two feet above his body. His body would decompose, undisturbed by discovery.

Ellie chewed her nails down to the quick over the following days, expecting and waiting for someone to file a missing person report. A friend, a coworker, or a family member, but nobody came forward. As much as it had hurt Ellie when Derek said no one was going to look for her, it pleased her that nobody cared enough about Derek now to search for him.

Cleanup of the apartment was more complicated. Margaret and Molly moved the dead woman's body to another location. They were careful not to leave their DNA on her. They left her in the woods near a hiking trail. It hurt Ellie to think of the poor woman's family never having closure on who killed their loved one. But they would at least have some closure in knowing that she was dead and not suffering somewhere. Someone found her body the next day. The police had their news conferences, remarking that the woman's injuries were consistent with an animal attack. They warned against entering the forest at night and set up traps to capture the animal that didn't exist.

Ellie watched the news conference with the other coven members. They were not safe, not yet. They waited for the slip-up, the small part of their plan they hadn't accounted for. The mistake that would expose them. But luck was on their side, and the police soon moved on. There were no more murders reported for a few weeks, and the press died down. They had gotten away with it this time.

Then there was River. She'd been angry with him for saving her. She had been ready to die. In the few moments where she clung to the in-between, a certain peace settled within her. When she thought of it in the days that followed, she had trouble remembering what had happened. It came back like a dream. The scene fell through her fingers like sand. All that remained were the smallest, insignificant molecules that couldn't paint the complete picture in her mind.

When she awoke to see River smiling down at her, his eyes full of tears, she thought she'd died. This was her afterlife, to gaze into the eyes of her lover. Happy for eternity.

The image quickly warped as his face grew pale and her body became wet with his blood. In the aftermath, more questions loomed in her head, each one more horrifying than the next. Did they resurrect her? Would the creatures now follow her? If River died, would she go too?

Using the key Molly gave her, Ellie let herself in. She'd been there so often over the past two weeks that she'd learned the entire layout of the house. Two tense weeks filled with close calls, but River held on.

The spell transferred her wounds to his body, only less so. Ellie didn't remember much of the pain, and all that remained was a scar on her abdomen. Yet River's wound seemed deep and fatal to her, but Molly assured her it wasn't.

Molly explained they hadn't resurrected her. She wasn't dead when they bound his soul to hers. They were tied, but not in the same way as she'd been with Derek. They used a different spell, and so the consequences would be different.

"I don't think we have to worry about afterlife vultures and transformations this time," Lola explained one night to Ellie after a particularly scary night.

River's breathing had become labored, gasping for air as if none existed in the room. He stabilized as the hours stretched into the night, but Ellie couldn't sleep after. Lola stayed over, keeping her company.

Lola had a calming presence; her touch acted like a balm as she rubbed Ellie's back. "You're fated to be with him. I wonder how that changes the spell."

"What do you mean?" asked Ellie.

"The spell we used was one from my family's book. It's a love spell, although most people tie their souls to somebody who wants nothing to do with them. I wonder how it will change tying two people who were already destined to be with one another."

"If one of us were to die, would the other die too?" asked Ellie.

"I don't know. My guess is yes. But let's not test it," said Lola with a smile.

Molly kept River at her home. Her knowledge of herbs kept infection at bay with her poultices. Molly was downright maternal with Ellie. Asking her if she'd eaten, slept, or done anything besides worry over River.

"He's going to be fine," Molly told her one night at four in the morning when she caught Ellie awake by his bedside. "You're not going to make him better by staring at him."

"I know that," she protested.

"And you won't feel good tomorrow if you don't sleep!"

Ellie let Molly steer her towards her guest room and flopped down on the comfortable bed. She was thankful to Molly. She loved and cared for her as if she'd been in the coven since its inception. Ellie wondered how she had survived as long as she had in the outside world without a coven. Sure, they were helpful in a time of crisis, but their companionship lightened the load she hadn't realized she carried.

However, the coven wasn't the only thing helping Ellie through. One night, as Ellie kept her usual post by River's bedside, she sensed it. Her mother's signature again, vibrating in the room. It enveloped Ellie with hope. They were protected. She knew then he would live.

Ellie bounded up the stairs, her heart leaping in her chest. She wondered whether he was still awake. Molly had sent the message fifteen minutes ago. After two weeks of waiting, worrying, and praying to any spirit and deity that would listen, she nearly cried as she saw River sitting up in bed.

"Ellie," he said, with a wide smile on his face.

She ran, tripping into his arms. He winced; Ellie apologized, trying to pull back, but he wouldn't let her. Keeping her wrapped in his arms and kissed her head. She melted into his chest, the herbal smell of one of Molly's poultices clinging to his clothes and bandages.

"I missed you," he said, trying his best to hold her tighter. "I thought I was dead," he started.

Ellie wanted to stop him. He was nowhere near dead, and she was alive thanks to him. Yet she knew from her own experience that it was important to talk about it. When she was close to death, she had spent an afternoon talking about it with Violet, trying to make sense of the experience.

"What did you see?" she asked him.

His hand stroked her hair, his eyes distant. "I saw you. But they weren't dreams exactly. I saw you crying. Standing over me, all quiet but sad."

"Maybe you were seeing me while I was here, waiting for you to wake up."

"You didn't leave?" he asked.

"Not if I could help it. Molly's sick of me now, I'm sure."

"I doubt it." He smiled, his hands traveling up her arms, embracing her as hard as he physically could. His caress lacked the strength he normally had when he held her, but all that would get better in time.

"Everything's okay now," said Ellie. "Derek's gone."

"Everything worked out," said River as if he still didn't believe it.

"Yes," she reassured him.

"I'm not used to everything working out for me. I thought for sure this would be like everything else. I thought I would lose you."

"You didn't lose me," she said.

"No," he whispered, "I didn't." He lifted himself to kiss her, and while Ellie worried about him overexerting himself, River had no such hesitations. His lips pressed urgently, and Ellie relished the feel of his tongue on hers.

"I saw something else," he said, pulling away breathlessly. His beard had grown while he was out, and Ellie liked how he looked with it. "We were at the morgue, and we had just been attacked by one of those things. I couldn't see them before, but I could see them in my dream. They were like enormous birds. With these horrible faces. And you were crying. You were helping me with my wounds. And then you kissed me."

"Um..."

"And I had another one. Of us in a club, and then we were in the alley. I'm not sure how detailed you want me to get."

Ellie blushed, and River laughed, kissing her again. This time, his lips traveled down her jaw, distracting her from what she wanted to say. But Ellie pushed him away. River protested clearly not interested in an apology. He tried pulling her in again for another kiss, but Ellie placed her hands on his chest, pushing him lightly down.

"I'm sorry. I forgot to tell you with everything happening so fast. But I erased your memory. I didn't want to bring you into my mess, and I thought it was the best thing to do."

"In some ways, I think they were still there, deep in my memory. Or else why would I have dreamed about it?"

"I meant to tell you."

"Will you ever do it again?"

"Erase your memory?" she asked.

"Yes."

"Never."

"Good, because I never want to lose another minute of my memory with you."

"Well, you're going to have a lot more now," she smiled.

"We have all the time in the world."

EPILOGUE

Spring thawed the early March snow, and the steady drip from the gutters woke Ellie up. She climbed out of bed and stretched in her red robe. It hiked higher, exposing her thigh, and River, half-asleep, reached up to touch it.

"Where are you going?" he asked, his voice gravelly in the morning.

"Coffee," mumbled Ellie, pulling away from his grasp. She sidestepped a few boxes that blocked her way out of their room.

Their room. She loved the way it sounded in her head. She walked through the hallway in *their home* and walked into *their kitchen.*

River had had the foresight to unpack the box that had the coffeemaker and coffee the night before. Ellie set it to percolating while she searched the boxes around her for a coffee mug.

There was peace in the morning. The birds chirped at the sun outside the kitchen window. She never knew that her life could be like this, calm and content.

River walked into the kitchen not long after her, stretching and yawning all the while.

"What are you looking for?" he asked.

"Mugs. Do you remember what box we put them in?"

"No," he laughed. He started searching himself, taking every moment he could to touch her. Her arms, her back, her face, her hands. Ellie tried slapping him away, but he was insistent.

"We'll never find it at this rate," she protested.

"Forget the coffee," he said.

"I need coffee," she laughed. "I need to wake up."

"I can wake you up," River said, smiling. Ellie laughed, her breath catching as his hands slipped beneath her pajama bottoms.

"No underwear?" he asked, cupping her sex. "Did you think you would get lucky last night?" He teased, kissing her neck. They had been so tired after moving boxes all day that they both had fallen asleep almost instantly.

Ellie pulled away. "I don't remember where I packed my underwear."

"Thank God for that," said River, slipping his finger between her folds. She shivered as his fingers entered her, the temperature difference between them striking.

River pushed her back, her ass meeting the counter. He placed his hands around her waist and helped hoist her up to sit on the countertop. He kissed her deeply, his lips slow and lazy against hers. His hands gripped the waistband of her pajama bottoms, and she lifted her hips to help him take them off.

Her own fingers played with his waistband, tugging at the strings to undo them. When they fell, she pulled away laughing when she realized he had no underwear either.

"Where's your underwear?" she asked.

"I was hoping to get lucky last night."

Her laugh reverberated around the room, an echo bouncing amongst the empty space. "Oh please, you were dead asleep when I got into bed last night."

"Mmm, a man can still hope. We haven't christened our home yet," his voice sounded harsh, and he rubbed his cock against her folds.

Her warm wetness spread between them; she was only growing wetter as the head of his cock stroked her clit.

"Do you know of a priest that'll bless it?" It was a miracle she still formed words.

"That's not the blessing I was thinking about," he laughed. He pressed himself against her. She threw her head back, biting her lips from crying out. It took her by surprise. His girth stretched her out. She hadn't been ready, but now that he was inside her, she settled around him. He pulled out halfway and harshly pushed back in. Ellie bit her lip again, her hands holding on to the counter, trying not to be pushed too far back from him.

"Don't do that," said River.

"Do what?" asked Ellie breathlessly.

"I don't want you to stop yourself from screaming. I see you biting your lip. You want to cry out, don't you? I'm making you feel good, aren't I?" A thrust punctuated each sentence. Ellie tasted blood now. They had gotten complaints from some of River's neighbors at his apartment since she had moved in. One of the main reasons they had decided that they needed to buy their own home as quickly as possible.

"Scream for me, Ellie."

His body tensed up with each steady and hard thrust of his hips. The sound of his body hitting against hers echoed through their near-empty house. She couldn't hold back anymore. She met each thrust with a shivered moan that made River thrust harder and harder.

He leaned down and pulled away her shirt and robe to kiss her breasts. His tongue lapped at her nipple and sucked gently. Ellie felt herself getting close. The gentleness of his sucking in opposition to the hardness of his thrusts pushed her closer.

She came hard; her back arching away from his supplicating mouth. River held himself inside of her, no longer moving. He groaned as her core clenched around his cock. He pulled her back to him to kiss her. Ellie kissed him slowly, her orgasm making her limbs languid and heavy.

River waited a moment. His hands traveled to her back, stroking it in slow circles. He was still hard inside her. She didn't know what he was waiting for. She lifted her head to meet his eyes.

"Are you okay?" she asked. He held her gaze and pushed back the hair from her face.

"I love you," he said.

"I love you too," said Ellie, with a kiss.

He let his hands fall on her thighs, and he grabbed her calves to wrap around his waist. Ellie wrapped her arms around his neck. River moved his hands to the bottom of her ass and hoisted her up. She sucked in air as her clit rubbed a little up. She was sensitive, and each step towards the couch teased her clit. River sat down, keeping Ellie on his lap.

Ellie smiled, leaning forward to kiss him again. His hands stayed around her hips, squeezing her fat as she moved against him. She rocked her hips. Her sensitive clit aching at the smallest of movements. River smirked, his fingers finding her clit. He stroked it in time with her hips, and Ellie felt her edge coming closer.

She threw her head back. Not yet. She wanted to come with him. But she would come too quickly if he continued on her clit. Her fingers scrambled to pull out his hand, but River pushed it back.

Ellie could be stubborn, too. She grabbed his wrist and pulled it next to his head on the couch. She found his other wrist and placed it next to his head as well. River could easily overpower her, she knew that, but he played along. She lifted her hips and slammed down on his shaft. She could tell River liked it by the way he closed his eyes and leaned back on the couch.

Ellie smiled to herself, resisting the urge to bite his exposed neck. She lifted her hips again and started to ride him vigorously. He moaned at her movement, whimpering as he came close to coming.

"Wait," he pushed his wrists off the couch, placing them around her face to kiss her. But Ellie didn't want to wait. Her orgasm was on the cusp. The sensation grew with every bounce on his cock. She wanted him to come with her. She needed it. River's hips took over, and he grabbed her waist as he fucked harder into her.

Ellie closed her eyes and was surprised by the sound of her own scream as she came. River came almost immediately after, and his cock pulsed within her. His hands wrapped around her body, pulling her closer to him.

They sat there for a moment, letting their breaths and heart rates return to normal. Ellie sighed against his neck, happy.

She could imagine a lifetime of this. A lifetime of lazy Sunday sex. A lifetime of peaceful love.

She had searched and searched for years for a slice of home. She found a home with the coven. And as River pushed back the hair from her face to kiss her again, she knew she had found it with him.

* * *

Afterword

Thank you so much for reading and I hope you enjoyed it! Please consider leaving a review as it helps a lot!

If you want to know what's next for Ellie and River, you can subscribe to my newsletter at https://www.sulaalba.com/newsletter for a free second epilogue.

About the Author

Sula Alba is a paranormal romance author living in the deserts of the Southwest.

When not writing, she loves to photograph her cats laying in the sun, baking and reading.

www.ingramcontent.com/pod-product-compliance
Lightning Source LLC
Chambersburg PA
CBHW020150310726

48970CB00006B/2087